MIDLIFE WOLF PACK

ACCIDENTAL ALPHA · BOOK 2

CARISSA ANDREWS

DEDICATION

*To all you mommas out there who are doing your thing
and still able to hang on to a shred of sanity.*

I see you.

CHAPTER 1

THE BEST PERSON FOR THE JOB

ELLA

Rage-painting should be an Olympic sport.

If it was, I'd be crowned Queen, for sure.

I wipe the sweat from my brow with the back of my hand and keep going. Come hell or high-water my bedroom will be painted tonight. But so help me, if I catch wind of another anxious thought from someone in the pack about how long it's taking me to pick my Beta, I'm gonna lose my mind.

It's not as if stepping into the role of Alpha for a *freakin' werewolf pack* is all easy breezy, Covergirl shit.

I mean, until a few weeks ago, I didn't even know werewolves were a thing.

Color me *mind-blown*.

In fact, back then, my biggest concern was whether or not moving to Oregon was far enough from the ex. Or if I could keep my two kids from slapping each other silly.

Now, all eyes are on me as the first female Alpha in generations and it's like they're expecting me to be their goddamn messiah. Well, either that or mess things up royally. Evidently, werewolves can be as sexist as the rest of the world.

I have no idea how to live up to the expectations swirling around me and I'm beginning to think this whole thing was a ridiculously bad idea. Not that I had much choice in the matter.

I wonder if she'll announce her choice by the full moon.

The thought barrels at me from Seth and I ground my teeth together.

Damn, this is getting old.

It wouldn't be so bad if I could get control of my mind and learn to filter how much of their thoughts I allow to flow to me. So far, that's proven difficult.

Which basically means, I'm gonna be driven mad as a hatter—and no one is gonna like that version of me. It's like when the kids were little and they thought they could wear me down by asking for something over and over and over. They learned very quickly that kind of thing had the opposite effect on me.

The difference here is that the pack members aren't *actually* asking me their questions. They're asking them of each other—or in their own minds.

But lord, they have *loud* minds.

I feel their apprehension like it's my own and it's putting me on edge. Not to mention, making me question myself.

It's not a fun feeling.

Sighing, I dunk my paint roller into the tray and make a mental note to pour more in soon. I slap the roller to the wall, continuing to rage-roll the dark lavender paint across the final beige surface left in our new home.

It's taken me two weeks of unpacking, painting, and all-around set-up to make it to the final room —*my bedroom*. It feels good to transform my personal space into something I resonate with.

God knows the ex would never have let me paint the bedroom walls purple. He would have laughed in my face and proceeded to paint it another shade of white because he was boring and lacked any kind of imagination.

Oh, if he could see me now.

"Mom, we're out of milk," Asher says, standing in the doorway. He leans against the frame, taking in the color of the room. Then, without a word, he nods in approval.

Smart kid.

"Wanna take my keys and run to the store?" I ask, returning my gaze to the wall and continuing on my mission.

At least the repetitive motion is keeping my hands busy.

"Not overly," he mutters. The glance I throw over my shoulder must clue him into my mood because he shifts upright and stares at me with wide brown eyes.

"I mean, I guess I can."

"Excellent," I say, continuing to spread happy purple across the wall.

"Need anything else?"

"Just peace and quiet," I sigh.

It's more about the voices in my head than the kids at this point, but a little less bickering and YouTube videos being played at max volume wouldn't go amiss.

"What's going on?" Avery asks.

She steps up beside her brother as I turn around with the paint roller raised in my hand like a torch.

"Your brother is going to the grocery store. Evidently, we're out of milk."

Avery slides her gaze to her brother and her eyebrows skirt her hairline. She lowers her voice conspiratorially and says, "She's letting you take the Highlander?"

Asher shrugs. "I guess?"

Avery grabs him by the shoulders and half-pushes him into the landing area outside of my bedroom door.

"Dude, don't stand around looking like you don't know where the door is. Take those keys and run, man. What's wrong with you?" she hisses.

I shake my head and return to painting. Of course, half of me has tuned into their conversation with rapt attention.

Thank you, super-sensitive werewolf hearing.

"Yeah, but it's not like I get to go anywhere fun. It's

the *grocery store*," he retorts, mimicking the same level of a rushed whisper as his sister.

"That doesn't mean you can't go other places. It's a vehicle, Asher. It goes where you make it to go," Avery says.

My expression deadpans but I keep painting.

She's not wrong and I guess, when I was a kid, any chance to get out of the house was a chance to stretch my wings of independence. I typically found myself at the mall or the bookstore, though.

Maybe a boyfriend's house or two...but we won't talk about that.

"Have you seen the size of this town? Where would I even go?" Asher snorts.

"Who cares? *Anywhere*," Avery says. "If I was old enough to drive, I'd go *exploring*."

I set the paint roller down and walk to the doorway, planting a hand on my hip.

The two of them glance in my direction like they were in the middle of planning a heist.

"If you're going to make plans to go all wild child on me, can you at least *not* do it right outside my door? I've got enough to worry about right now between the pack's craziness and the full moon coming up..." I mutter, running a hand over my face. "I gotta figure out a way to rein it all in."

"We should host a party," Asher announces.

Surprised, I glance at him through my splayed fingers. "Excuse me?"

5

"We're new in town and you've got this differ-ent..."—Asher narrows his eyes—"*job thing.*"

"Is there a point buried in there?" I ask, dropping my hand and slowly arching an eyebrow.

"I just thought it would help you relax and maybe connect with your, uh, *team*. I mean, it's almost the Fourth of July..." Asher mutters, running his hand across the back of his neck. "Forget it."

I hold a hand out. "No, maybe you're on to some-thing, kid."

"He is?" Avery says, shock reverberating in her tone.

"Well, yeah. I've been trying to figure out how to get to know everyone and help them get to know us. I mean, it's weird—" I say, letting my words peter out. I haven't really talked a whole lot about my transition to the kids because I want their life to stay as normal as possible. But it's pretty hard not to notice the gigantic pink elephant in the room when it's stomping all over your living room.

"You're telling us," Avery whispers under her breath.

She hasn't been thrilled with things since I wolfed out and the last thing I want to do is kick her anxiety into high gear.

"I think it's cool. I mean, Mom's basically a *badass*," Asher says, pride riding his words.

Despite the swell of appreciation, I fire back, "Language."

He zips his mouth tight and holds his hands up. "Well, you are."

"Regardless," I say, shooting him a knowing look.

Suddenly, the hairs on the back of my neck and arms rise and a thrill races through my entire being. I turn to face my front door.

Stone's on his way here.

"Oh man, she's doing it again," Avery grumbles.

I glance back at her. "Doing what?"

She rolls her eyes like a true teen. "You're making a goofy face and reacting to stuff we can't even—"

The doorbell rings and she presses her lips tight, raising her arms as if she rests her case.

"It's just Stone," I say, walking around them and hitting the stairs.

"Asher, take me with you. I don't wanna be home if they're giving each other the oogly eyes," Avery declares.

"Yeah, me either," Asher says, following behind me. "Come on."

My midsection flutters and I inhale sharply. I'm not so sure being alone in the house with Stone is such a good idea.

I couldn't be held responsible for my actions.

By the time I open the front door, Asher has already grabbed the keys to the SUV.

"Hey, Stone," he says, stepping sideways as he exits the open door and continues onward.

Avery follows after him, waving awkwardly as she goes by.

"Be careful," I call out after them. Sighing, I wave Stone in. "Kids."

The smile that creeps across Stone's face is the stuff that makes my heart skip beats and my legs turn into jelly. Even after the past few weeks, I have to pinch myself when I think about this guy somehow finding himself in my bizarre orbit. Or maybe it's more accurate that I've found myself in his...

He laughs, glancing over his shoulder. "Where are those two off to so fast?"

"Grocery store, *supposedly*. But I have a feeling the majority of it will be joy riding," I mutter, trying to ignore the panic those words invoke. "They better at least fill up the gas tank on their way home."

Stone nods, clasping his hands behind his back. His light gray button-down shirt is rolled up at the sleeves, showcasing the tattoos on his forearms in a way that stirs my insides. It also fits snugly across his broad shoulders and chest, and tapering nicely as it tucks into his dark denim jeans.

I sigh contently. He's a beauty to behold, that's for sure.

"So, to what do I owe the pleasure?"

Swiping a stray hair out of my face with the back of my hand, I realize I must be a hot mess. I have paint clothes on, which consists of old sweats and a tattered t-shirt that says, "And she said *'fuck this shit,'* then lived happily ever after." To top it off, purple paint is splattered across my fingertips and goodness knows where else.

Stone's emerald gaze sweeps from the top of my wild hair to my toes. Then, he steps forward, rubbing his thumb across my cheek. "You have a little paint..."

"Yeah, I've been finishing up my bedroom," I explain, trying not to feel disappointed when his hand leaves my face.

We've been keeping things between us on a simmer but there's some red-hot magma burning under the surface and every time we're in the same room, it threatens to boil over. I keep trying to rationalize that now's not the time to dive headlong into a full-blown relationship but the rest of me isn't always in agreement on that matter.

Stone steps around me, taking in the rest of the house. It's been a few of days since he was here and the last of the boxes were unpacked in that span.

"The house is looking great. You sure work fast when you want to," he says with a hint of sarcasm as he returns his gaze to me.

I cross my arms. "Was that a dig at my decision-making skills on the Beta position, Mr. Lachlan? Please tell me you're not going to join in on that bandwagon."

Even as the words escape my lips, in the back of my mind, I hope it wasn't actually a dig at the progression of our relationship.

A broad grin creeps across his features and he huffs

a laugh. "Maybe a little. I can't help it. You've been ruminating so loudly about it, I had to poke fun."

Despite the relief that washes over me, my face crumples. "I've been that loud?"

"Well, I don't know if *everyone* is picking up on it, but I certainly have," he whispers, taking a step toward me. "What's bothering you so much?"

I drop my head back and groan. "*Everything.*"

"You'll need to be more specific." He chuckles.

Lifting my head, I stare into his eyes for the longest time, wishing I could find the right words to relay all the worries I've been fending off.

Finally, I sigh. "I don't want the pack to think my feelings for you will influence my decision. I want to make a good impression and—"

Surprise flashes through those green eyes of his. "If you're worried about that, don't pick me."

"But you were the last Beta. Well, the last non-homicidal Beta. Wouldn't that make you the best, er —*person* for the job?"

Stone places his warm hands on my shoulders. "Only the Alpha can decide who the best person for the job is. You have a different energy than Doug and your leadership should reflect that. If you're hesitating, it means you need to stop letting others influence your decision and trust your own."

I narrow my gaze. "See, isn't that the sort of thing a Beta would say?"

Again, he chuckles. "Perhaps. But so would a good friend. Or..."

"Or...?" I hold my breath, watching his every move.

"Whatever it is we are," he finishes softly. His words are thoughtful but they hold the same silent question that's been lingering in my mind.

My breath hitches and my mouth goes dry. "What do *you* think we are?"

His lashes flutter across his cheeks. Then he slides his hands down to my upper arms. Creases form across his forehead and I lean in, trying desperately to tune into his thoughts. However, he has them locked up far better than I can seem to be able to do.

Finally, he says, "I'm not sure what we are just yet, Ella. But I'm looking forward to seeing where things lead."

CHAPTER 2
WELL, THAT WAS AWKWARD

ELLA

What in the hell do you say to something like that?

Yeah, me too?

I mean, *of course*, me too.

Lord, I'm so far out of my dating comfort zone.

"Uh, do you want to come up to my bedroom?" I blurt out.

The comment seemed reasonable in my head, but the moment the words have sprung from my mouth, I realize how they could be taken.

Stone's eyes widen and my heartbeat kicks up another notch.

Did I honestly just say that?

I clear my throat and try again. "You know, to see how it's turning out?"

Stone blinks quickly then tips his chin upward. "Oh, right. Sure, I'd love that." He takes a step back, turning his palm upward and thrusting it in the direction of the stairs. "Lead the way."

Heat creeps into my cheeks, and I turn on my heel, hoping to get out in front before he can notice. I roll my eyes at myself.

The kids definitely had the right idea. Witnessing their hopeless mother fumble with flirting would be painful to watch.

When I reach the top of the stairs, I spin around. "Now, promise me, even if you don't like what you see, you will lie to me."

Stone's forehead creases. "Excuse me?"

I can't help but giggle at the bewildered expression on his face. "Just say you like it."

He snickers under his breath. "I make no such promises. I am nothing if not honest."

"Hmmm." I narrow my gaze, shifting my lips slightly to one side, trying to decide if it's wise to bring him in here so soon.

I mean, if he doesn't like it or acts like the ex... Do I want to be disillusioned by him so soon?

I suppose it's too late to turn back now.

Without another word, I spin on my heel and continue to the bedroom. But as I enter the space, all thoughts of the renovation flee my brain and instead, I relive the first time he was in this room...

Once again, my heart feels like it might beat itself out of my chest.

Wolves may have no shame or vanity about being

naked but he sure burned the memory of his form into my sex-deprived brain. It's all I've been able to think about when I've been alone with my thoughts...and alone in this room.

I shudder away the sensations the memory invokes in my body and catch him eyeing me from the doorway. Clearing my throat, I hold my arms out wide and pray like hell he couldn't hear those thoughts.

"Well, what do you think? I mean, obviously, it's not done yet," I mutter, pointing back at the unfinished wall behind me.

"This is..." he begins, taking a step into the room. His eyes take in everything as they flit from the bed, to the walls, to the window, and back to the bed.

I squint at him, waiting for him to tarnish the armor I've built up in my head.

When he catches my eye, he laughs. "This is very *you*."

My heart beams. Like actually, full-on *beams*.

He's barely known me for a month and he already knows what's *me*.

Okay, armor officially still intact.

Nodding to myself, I press my hands to my hips and admire the room. I have to admit, it's turning out even better than I had envisioned. Once the purple walls are done, I'll be adding wood paneling to the lower half. It will truly make the room look like a grandiose oasis. At least, that's what I keep telling myself.

Grinning like a kid, I say. "Like me... I guess that's sorta the point, right?"

"Yep, I believe it is." His grin is broad but he lingers back a bit, almost as if he's not overly comfortable coming all the way into the room.

"Okay, so tell me the truth. Do *you* like it?" I ask, unable to stop the hint of worry from bleeding into my words. "It's kinda bold."

"I do, actually," he says, spinning in a slow circle. "It reminds me of the color of night. It's peaceful...but *mysterious* at the same time."

Screwing up my face, I tip my head to the side. "Huh, never thought of that. I just liked the color."

"That doesn't surprise me in the least," Stone says, maneuvering back to the doorway. He leans against the doorframe in the same stance Asher had done earlier.

"You know, you never answered me earlier," I say, realizing we never really established a reason for his visit.

Confusion crops up on his face. "What didn't I answer?"

"Why are you here, Stone?" I ask, shaking my head. "I mean, it's not that isn't great to see you. Obviously, it's great to—uh...see you." I butt the palm of my hand against my forehead and mumble, "Lord help me. I sound like an idiot."

Again, I feel the color creep into my cheeks. I can only imagine what he thinks...

Because I feel drawn to you.

I glance up. The thought isn't mine and I blink at him, realizing he let this one slip past his iron guard.

His eyebrows tug in and he swallows hard.

"I just wanted to check in to see if you needed any help," he says, a slight grin playing at the edge of his lips.

My insides flutter again and I feel a little better —*lighter*.

"Well, I'm almost done," I say, pointing back at the nearly finished wall.

He nods, shifting slightly. "I see that."

Come on, Ella. Steer this ship away from Awkwardville and fast.

"You know, come to think of it, there is something you could help with," I say, tapping my lips with my index finger.

His gaze falls to my fingertips but jolts back up to my eyes. "What's that?"

"Do you think the pack would like a party?" I ask, steepling my fingers and strumming my fingertips together.

"A party?"

"Yeah, Asher brought it up and the more I think about it, the more I think it could be a great idea. The pack doesn't really know us and we don't really know them. I mean, I have a much better sense of each of them than I did before I"—my gaze softens—"*shifted*."

Stone's eyebrows rise into his dark hairline.

"A party might work," he says, crossing his arms over his torso. "What kind of party were you thinking of?"

My shoulders relax a bit and I let out the breath I was holding. "Well, it's almost the Fourth of July. We could do a big barbecue—burgers and brats or something. Maybe even have some fireworks? You know, the kind that won't blow up someone's hands or anything—I'm thinking of Asher there. Basically, just kick back with some music and drinks. What do you think? Too dorky?" I bite down on the side of my lip and wait for his response.

"I think that sounds like a great idea. I can't say it's something any of the other Alphas would have thought to do."

"Does that mean it's dumb?" I ask, narrowing my gaze.

"No, not at all. Just like this room—it means *it's you.* They'll get a better feel for the leadership you're going to bring because of it," Stone says. The crow's feet beside his eyes deepen with his smile letting me know he's the kind of guy who's smiled a lot in his life.

For the second time in the past few minutes, my heart soars.

Without thought, I rush over to him, wrapping my arms around his neck.

"Thank you," I whisper, my lips brushing against the side of his cheek.

He smells like the woods after a good rain—with

maybe a hint of shaving cream. I inhale deeply, wishing I could revel in it without it being totally weird.

After a couple of seconds, his arms wrap around my waist, tugging me closer to him. I melt into his body, pressing myself against him.

Damn, he gives good hugs.

"I don't know what I did but I'll take it."

"You were being you," I whisper, trying desperately to keep myself in check.

When I pull back, I tuck a stray hair behind my left ear. He watches me closely but the energy in the room has shifted between us. There's something else there —*an electric current*—that wasn't present moments ago.

Stone slides his right hand alongside my jaw. Before I have a chance to question it, his lips crush down on mine, and all sense of reality flees from my brain.

I breathe him in, responding to his kiss like it's the one thing in this whole world that could save me from my miserable life. My hands fly to his hair and I run my fingertips through it, tugging gently.

A growl erupts from deep in his chest and it excites me more than makes sense.

Then his hands drop to my waist, sliding just under the hem of my shirt. They linger on either side of me, the warmth from his hands radiating into my skin and eliciting a moan.

How he can do that and not even touch my more sensitive parts, I'll never know.

Feverishly, I work at the buttons of his shirt, trying to get them open without breaking them.

His tongue skates across my lower lip and my breath hitches.

In a swift movement, he slides his hands upward and lifts the shirt from my body. I wiggle out of it, returning quickly to his shirt and sliding it over his shoulders. My palms drift over the firm muscles of his chest and shoulders, then across the backs of his arms.

God, they feel as good as they look.

For a moment, he watches me with a feral, animalistic glow in his eyes. Like he'll claim me for his own right here and now.

He returns his mouth to mine as my hands roam over his torso. I need to feel every inch of him. He does the same, palming me over my bra. The sensation drives me wild and all I can think is how fast I want the damn thing off.

I reach around, unhooking it with one hand so I can wiggle out of it. It slides off my body, landing on the floor between us. Stone takes a beat, his hungry gaze taking me in before his palms return to my body, sending electric currents that spread out from each point of contact. His fingertips pinch and pull, forcing another moan from my lips.

I drop my hands to the front of his jeans, unbuttoning them, and sliding the zipper down. He shivers under my touch and I press the palm of my hand against the heat pulsating just beneath the fabric.

Another deep growl rumbles through his chest and he lifts me clear off my feet, carrying me to the bed. He drops me down on my back, spreading my legs beneath him. With a slow, rocking movement, he tips his hips and presses his bulge against me.

I swear to all that's holy, I have to close my eyes before they roll back into my head.

There's too much fabric between us and I scramble again, trying desperately to yank off his jeans. There needs to be less clothing...

However, he suddenly pulls back, tipping his chin down, and breathing heavily.

"Shit. We should stop..." Stone whispers, gathering my hands together and binding them between us.

I blink back in surprise. My entire body is a live wire right now and I can't even imagine stopping things.

For a moment, I wait, dumbfounded, as I try to let whatever feelings are coming up for him to sort themselves out. When he doesn't say anything else, I pull my hands from his and place them on either side of his face, forcing him to look at me.

His emerald gaze pleads with me to understand— but I don't. I don't know what we're bargaining for.

"I'm old enough to make my own decisions, you know," I say, trying to tame my heart and the sensations rolling through my body.

He chuckles, rubbing the back of his hand across my cheekbone. "I know that. It's just—"

The front door opens and slams shut.

"See, I told you it wouldn't be that bad," Avery says. "It was fun to get out and drive, wasn't it?"

"Yeah, but it would have been better without having to go to the mall. That was pointless," Asher responds.

"True. I can't believe they close so early," Avery mutters.

However, the crinkling of plastic bags tells me they got more than just milk while they were out.

I glance up into Stone's apologetic smile. At least he had heard the two of them coming because my wolf-senses had left me totally in the dark.

Or maybe I learned how to tune them out.

"Shit," I mutter, dropping back in the bed and covering my face with my hands. "Worst timing ever."

CHAPTER 3

REPRESENTATION

ELLA

Clementine drops into the seat opposite me and slides a white coffee cup across the table. She's dressed in jeans and a vibrant shirt with orange, green, and yellow splattered across it. As if it didn't scream "look at me" loud enough, her nails are painted yellow to match. Interestingly, her wild brown hair accentuates the look, rather than detracts from it.

"So, my dear, what's on your mind?" she asks, taking a long draw from her own mug.

I shift my gaze to her expectant green eyes and my mind goes completely blank.

The only thing I can muster up are dirty thoughts about her brother—which of course I won't bring up. Getting interrupted by the kids last night did a number on my psyche and I can only imagine how Stone's doing. Poor guy.

So yeah, that's probably not the best conversation to have with her.

Instead, I pick up my cup with a smile and say, "Not much. I just needed to get out of my house for a bit. I'm supposed to start back at my job soon and once that happens, I'm sure I'll be homebound and doing research."

Clementine narrows her gaze and takes a sip of her cappuccino. "You write for a magazine, right? Which one is it again?"

I nod absently and take a quick sip of my black coffee. It's way too hot for consumption yet, so I purse my lips to fight off the sting and set the cup back down. "Yeah. Don't worry, most people forget what it is as soon as I say it. It's called *Pharma Formulary.* I write articles about medications and their interactions. It's a clinical magazine for pharmacists."

The corners of her lips tug downward but her eyebrows arch high in surprise. Then, she shakes her head. "Nope, pretty sure I never knew that." She chuckles under her breath and takes another sip. "Do you like the work?"

"It's okay, I guess. With the exception of the E.D. articles, it's pretty interesting stuff." I shrug.

"E.D.?"

I scrunch the side of my face. "Sorry, occupational hazard." Leaning in closer, I whisper, *"Erectile dysfunction."*

Her eyebrows shoot upward. "Ah... That must be..."

I shudder. "If I didn't have to write another E.D. article in all my life, I would die a happy woman."

"If E.D. didn't exist, every man could die happy, too," Clementine laughs. "So, how are the kiddos? They settling in okay?"

I squint, trying to ignore my mind as it dives back to the mad scramble to get dressed last night. *The traitor.*

Avery had been quick to climb the stairs and I'm pretty sure she knew something was up when my door quickly swung shut.

Clementine quirks an eyebrow.

I clear my throat. "Yeah, I think they're mostly okay. I mean, Avery still doesn't want to talk about the whole—" I lean in and whisper, *"wolf thing."*

"You know most of the people here are in the pack, right?" Clementine says, with a hint of a smirk. "We need to get you integrated more so you can tell."

Sighing, I glance around the room. There are roughly fifteen people in the coffee shop and she's not wrong. I just hadn't been paying much attention— what with my mind in the gutter.

Now that I tune in, I can sense the majority of them as part of the Black Crater Pack. Even if I haven't interacted one-on-one very much with most of them.

"Right," I mutter, taking another sip and floating my gaze around the room again. "I guess I'm still not used to any of this yet. It still feels like it should be a big secret."

A woman sitting alone in the corner catches my eye. She's Asian, with a petite build, and jet black hair that's cropped short on one side and semi-long on the other. Running along the side of her neck is some sort of tattoo but it's hard to see what it is from here. Her attention is turned toward the phone in her hand but something about her, maybe it's the energy or the aura she puts out, is interesting. It's like she's a rebel who's just ready to be unleashed.

"Who's that?" I ask, my curiosity getting the better of me.

She's not part of the pack, that much is clear, but for some reason, I can't stop staring. A niggling thought tickles at the back of my mind, telling me I should invite her to join us.

Clementine glances over her shoulder and shrugs. "Not sure. I don't think I've ever seen her before. Why?"

"No particular reason, I guess." I take another sip of my coffee, debating with myself on whether or not I should say hello. Returning my gaze to Clementine, I ask, "How about you? How have *you* been?"

Her head jangles on her neck as she feigns some sort of nonchalance. "Eh, fine. I'm glad the funeral is over and all that. Maybe now I can find some sense of normalcy."

"Finding a new normal is good," I whisper.

Clementine is strong, but I can only imagine how painful dealing with the loss of a husband would be to deal with. Well, a husband you still loved, at any rate. The last thing I want to do is stir up her feelings and make things worse.

"So, what about you? Have you and Stone figured your shit out yet?" Clementine asks, a mischievous sparkle flashing in her eye.

Gripping my cup tightly, I blink at her. "Figured our...?"

"You know, have you *sealed the deal?*" She laughs. "He's certainly got the air of a wolf ready to claim his mate."

"I, uh—" I stammer, searching for something to say.

Claim his mate?

She holds out a hand. "Don't get me wrong, I want no gory details. But I do like seeing my brother happy for a change. He deserves a little bit of joy after the past few years."

I tap the edge of my cup. "Things are...*good.* I think?"

"Why is that a question?" she asks, concern tightening her features.

My gaze extends past her and I tip my head back, looking at the poorly painted ceiling. "Because...*kids.*"

Clementine chuckles. "Ah, yes. Those demons with impeccable timing and obnoxious attitudes. What happened? Anything noteworthy that I won't be appalled to hear?"

When I remove my gaze from the ceiling, I squint at her. "Impeccable timing about sums it up."

She sticks out a tongue but nods. "Yeah, our kids had that knack as well."

"You and Doug have kids?" I ask, surprised.

"Oh, yeah," she laughs. "But it's been a minute. They're old now—with packs of their own."

"So, they're all wolves?"

She nods. "Every last one. It's in our bloodline, so..."

I tap the side of my coffee cup, trying to imagine what that would be like—having kids who were also werewolves. I'm not sure I'd want this life for my kids. It's weird enough that I've been thrust into it. If anything, I want them to lead as normal a life as possible—as far away from the potential dangers of this new life as they can.

"That must have been hard," I say before I think better of it.

Clementine shrugs. "It's all we ever knew."

I nod absently, my thoughts wrapped up in the idea of having kids who were also capable of turning into werewolves. I'm still not fully rooted in the realization that *I'm* able to shift yet.

"So, any idea on when you'll be selecting your Beta? The pack is certainly curious," she asks, smirking at me before she takes a long sip from her cup.

My expression flattens. "Not you, too."

A soft chuckle escapes her lips. "Honestly, I don't

care. Anyone you choose will be better than Silas. I just know the rest of the pack is anxious to know the dynamic."

I blow out a puff of air and lean back. "It's not as easy of a choice as the rest of the pack might think. The last thing I want to do is pick someone and have that decision undermine my leadership because they think favoritism is at work. Being a leader is hard."

Clem arches an eyebrow. "So, no to Stone, then?"

I rock my head from shoulder to shoulder. "Eh...?"

"Well, that is a surprise. I figured he'd be the obvious choice," she says.

"And therein lies the problem," I say. "Maybe I'm making too much out of this. Am—am I making too much out of this?"

"You're the only one who can decide your leadership, Ella. If you're hesitating with Stone, you need to trust that."

I snicker. "That's basically what *he said*, too."

"You talked to him about this?"

Nodding, I take another sip of my coffee. "Yeah. Last night before the...*impeccable timing.*"

"I see..."

"On the other hand, I don't want to take so long that the pack questions my decision-making abilities, either," I say, narrowing my gaze. "Hey, do you want to help me plan a party for the pack?"

"Yeah, that wouldn't be good," she begins, but her eyes widen. "Shoot, is that the time?" She pulls back her sleeve to check her watch and stands up. "Dammit, Ella, I gotta bug out. I totally spaced. I have an electrician coming over to help me hook up a dishwasher at the house."

"Oh, sorry. I shouldn't have kept you—" I mutter, standing up with her.

She shakes her hands in the air between us. "No, it wasn't you at all. I lost track of time. But to answer your question, *of course*. I'd love to help you plan a shindig for the pack. They won't know what hit them." She winks at me, then pats my shoulder as she walks on by. "I'll call you tomorrow."

Before I know it, Clementine has vacated the coffee shop. I sit back down in my seat, staring at my half-full cup.

"Alrighty, then," I mutter under my breath. "Guess it's just me and you."

Yet, as I say it, I glance back up, noticing again the woman in the corner. She's still sitting alone and still staring at her phone. However, the pull to talk to her hasn't diminished. I realize now, that in addition to the badassery in her vibe, there's also a sadness about her. It's not overpowering but enough that maybe a talk with a strange lady might cheer her up.

Without second-guessing it, I stand up and make my way over to her.

As I approach, she glances up with an expression of curiosity and confusion plastered across her face.

"Hi, there. I'm Ella. I—I'm new in town," I say, thrusting out my hand in offering.

She blinks at me for a beat but extends her hand as well. "Alanna."

"Nice to meet you, Alanna. Sorry, I hope you don't mind the intrusion. I just couldn't help but notice you were all alone—" I begin, realizing I sound like I'm trying to pick her up. An absurd laugh escapes my lips. "Sorry, I swear, I'm not trying to ask you on a date."

Alanna cracks a smile and it lights up her face. "I did wonder there for a minute."

"Truly, I just wanted to say hello. God, it's weird trying to make friends in your forties," I mutter, running a hand over my face.

She laughs softly. "Don't I know it?"

"So, are you new here, too?" I ask, trying to zoom past the awkwardness as fast as possible.

Alanna shakes her head. "No, I've lived in the area for a decade or so."

"Oh, that's nice. How do you like it?" I ask, clutching the back of the chair opposite her.

She hesitates for a moment, her gaze flitting around the room. Finally, she says, "It's good. *Quiet.*"

I nearly laugh out loud. Quiet isn't one of the adjectives I'd use for Black Crater, but then again, my circumstances are probably wildly different from hers.

"My kids and I moved here almost a month ago. It seems like a great place so far."

One of Alanna's dark eyebrows arches, and for a

moment, I swear she wants to say something. Instead, she simply nods her head in agreement.

"Well, it was nice to meet you, Alanna. I guess I won't keep you—" I say, jabbing my thumbs toward the direction I'd come.

A crease forms between her eyebrows but the smile hasn't faded from her lips. "It was nice to meet you, too, Ella. I'm sure we'll bump into each other again."

I grin, nodding. "I'd like that. Who knows? Maybe we'll even have a chat over coffee."

"A very real possibility," she laughs, returning her gaze to her phone.

I walk back toward the table Clementine and I had sat at. My coffee cup has been removed, likely by the barista, so I keep on walking toward the exit.

Right before I hit the door, a man in his mid-to-late-fifties grabs hold of my wrist, pulling me up short.

He tsks under his breath. "As Alpha, you should be more careful who you associate with. You represent the pack and you'd do well to remember that."

CHAPTER 4
THE AUDACITY OF SOME PEOPLE

ELLA

"Excuse me?" I say, yanking my hand from the man's clutches.

He's a wolf but not part of our pack. Yet, for some reason, his face is so familiar.

It doesn't take long for recognition to catch up and I understand why he's such an ass.

He's not a part of the pack now, but he was.

He's one of the men who stood by Silas—and was cast out because of it.

"You heard me," he mutters, his chin elevated and nostrils flaring.

My pulse hammers in my ears and I don't even bother to reel in the anger boiling under the surface. This guy either has a steel pair or a head full of rocks.

I bend down, leaning in as close as I dare. Lowering my voice to barely above a whisper, I say, "As an outcast, you'd do well to keep your opinions to yourself."

Even if I wasn't fully aware of the power that rides my words, and perhaps I'm not, their effect is evident immediately. Those in my pack who happen to be in the coffee shop, snap to attention, turning to face me. Their energy is instantly on alert and ready to step in, should I need them.

Those not in the pack—like this guy—cower slightly. He tries desperately to maintain his control, but after a moment, his eyes drop and he stares at the table.

Nodding to myself, I glance around the room, catching the eye of anyone who dares look me in mine. I may be taking some time to adjust to this new role, but if anyone thinks I'll be a pushover, they're in for a rude awakening.

When I catch Alanna's eye, a slow smirk spreads across her lips. I tip my head in her direction and walk straight out the door.

No one—not an ex-pack member, current pack member, or anyone else for that matter, will tell me who I can or cannot associate with.

Alanna might not be a wolf but who the hell cares? I wasn't one until a few weeks ago. My kids aren't...

When I reach my vehicle, I check my watch, debating if I should head back home or run some errands. It's the last day of my "moving vacation" and

I don't want to spend the whole day moping around the house or raging about the injustices of the world.

After putting the car into drive and meandering through the streets for a little while, I find myself in the parking lot of the Black Crater Educational Services building. I need to get Asher and Avery enrolled for fall and now's as good of a time as any to take care of that task. It's probably just a bunch of paperwork, anyway.

After the fiasco at the coffee shop, crossing an item off my ever-growing to-do list will help me feel more in control. Even though school won't start for another month and a half, it'll be a relief to set up tours of the schools so the kids can get oriented. When I was a student, I hated the feeling of a new school looming and not knowing what to expect.

The educational services building is a big brick beast, with marble embellishments along the corners and edges of doorways and windows. While it's got a business vibe to it now, the building also feels like it could have been a repurposed school.

The moment I step inside, the repurposed school vibe totally wins out. Some of the hallway sections still have old lockers clinging to the walls and the archaic bell system is evident near the ceiling. Interestingly, I'm hit with a wave of nostalgia.

While I'm sure going to school is slightly different now, I hope like hell the kids feel more at home here than they did in California.

I follow the signs guiding me toward the main office, but before I even open the door, my wolf senses perk up. I must have subconsciously gone on alert, thanks to that crazy guy.

There are two women inside and both are part of the pack. I wish I could place who they are, but unfortunately, the knowing is as far as my *knowing* goes.

I really need to throw that damn party. This is getting ridiculous.

I should know these people like they were family. Otherwise, how will they ever learn to respect me as their leader?

Throwing my shoulders back and chin up, I reach for the door handle and walk inside.

It's clear from the wide eyes and stiff backs, that the two of them sensed me coming, too.

"Hi, ladies," I say, waving and walking up to the counter. "I need to get my kids enrolled for fall. Is this the right place?"

The two of them exchange a quick glance.

"Yes, this is the place," the first woman says. She's slightly taller than the other one, with blond hair and bright blue eyes. She has a similar sense of style to Clementine—loud and proud. "We're thrilled to have you here. Had we known you were coming, we could have—"

Woman number two elbows her and she zips her lips.

I quirk an eyebrow, glancing between the two of them. "How would you have known I was coming?"

"Well, what I mean is, we could have had your packets put together before you arrived. I'd hate for you to waste so much time, Alpha," the blond says, dropping her gaze to the desk and bowing her head as if she had just been chastised.

"Good grief, don't worry about it. Until ten minutes ago, I didn't even know I was going to be coming here. Sometimes, you just gotta roll with the impulses, you know what I mean?" I say, trying to lighten the mood.

"Such powerful words," the blond says, nodding emphatically.

I narrow my gaze. "Oookay."

The second woman rolls her hazel eyes. "You'll have to forgive her. She's not used to dealing with the Alpha."

I chuckle under my breath. "Well, if that's all, I think we'll be just fine. I'm not used to being Alpha, yet. I think I gotcha beat."

"Yes, Alpha," the blond says, dropping her gaze like I just told her she needed to kiss my boots.

I glance at woman number two. Her dark eyebrows are knitted together.

Pretty sure she wants to tell the blond to get a grip. Heck, I'd like to tell her, too, but I get the impression that if I did, she might burst into tears. The last thing I need right now is an irate woman on my hands.

I clear my throat and focus on the second woman. "So,"—my gaze drops to her name badge—"*Erma*. I have a son who's going to be a senior this year and a daughter going into eighth grade. Any chance you can hook a girl up with enrollment for each of them?"

"Yes, Alpha," she says, holding her shoulders back and chin high. "I assume you'll want them enrolled in the pack's district?"

"It really is a better district," the blond says, leaning in like she's giving away trade secrets.

My eyes widen. I hadn't known there was a separate district for pack members. My god, I'm such a dunce when it comes to all of this.

Shaking my head, I say, "No, it's fine. They're not, you know..." My fingertips dance in the air by way of explanation.

"Oh, that doesn't matter. We wouldn't dream of alienating them just because they're, you know —*human*," Blondie says.

I eye her name badge, too, but it's hard to read her handwriting.

Blondie she'll remain.

"No, they'll be fine. Just regular, boring schools work. I mean, they're gonna hate it anyway. May as well hate it for all the normal reasons, right?" I laugh, swiping a hand in the air.

Erma's eyes widen and she presses her fingertips to her chest like I just offended her mother. "Why on earth would they hate our school?"

"I didn't mean—I just meant that they're human. So a normal school would be best for them. I appreciate the thought, though," I say, backpedaling since I'm getting the distinct impression things are going sideways fast.

"Ours is a better school. They'd be watched by the pack. No one would dare—"

"Seriously, I appreciate the concern, but the kids will be *fine*. Asher only has a year left. Public school isn't going to kill him. As for Avery—"

"We really do insist that they go to the pack's district. I know you're new here, but as Alpha, you'll want them to integrate with our children. If you segregate them, it could put a wedge between the pack members," Erma says, her expression suddenly stoic. "Not to mention, going to the public district could make them an easy target."

I narrow my gaze. "Excuse me?"

"She means they'd stand out as a vulnerability to you," Blondie says, trying to sound reasonable.

My gaze shifts back to Erma, who shuffles slightly and says, "If the kids go to the pack's district, they'll have friends in the pack. As a new Alpha, you're going to be a source of speculation. Other packs are going to be sniffing around and looking for your weaknesses. It's no secret kids are always a soft spot. All I meant was that if they have friends inside the pack, they'll have your kids' back."

"You won't be there to protect them twenty-four-seven," Blondie finishes.

My heartbeat thumps unevenly in my chest and the world feels like it's spinning. I had no idea when I came here just how complicated I'd make things for them. I can't even pick a goddamn school without it being a big fiasco that threatens my kids and their safety.

"Fuck," I mutter, placing my hands on the counter and dropping my head.

"So, the pack district?" Blondie asks, trying to sound chipper.

I scowl at her. "It would appear I don't have much of a choice, do I?"

"Well..." she sighs, then glances at her partner-in-crime.

"We do insist," Erma repeats, her voice low.

"Take care of it, then," I spit, turning on my heel.

If I'm being forced to put my kids in the pack's school, they can damn well figure out how to do it for me.

"Of course. We'll take care of everything," Blondie says behind me.

"Swell." I throw a hand up in lieu of a wave and walk out the door.

Anger and fear swirl in my stomach and the only thing I seem to be able to focus on is how much I've fucked things up.

I left one controlling, self-centered jerk only to land in another situation where I have no control.

How did that happen?

My phone vibrates in my front pocket and I pull it out.

"Ugh," I mutter, clutching the phone in my hand.

With the storm that's brewing inside me, I shouldn't even look at the stupid thing right now. Yet, as if possessed, I do exactly that. I unlock the phone and tap on the dumb message before I realize who sent it.

Without fail, I instantly regret the decision—as a part of me I knew I would.

Jesus Christ, Ella. Are you going to do your damn job and have the kids call me? It's been two weeks. What the hell am I paying child support for if they don't even talk to me?

I stare at the screen of my phone, dumbfounded by the audacity of people today. It's like there was some sort of memo that went out reminding them to be asshats.

Granted, I should have known this text was coming. It's been too quiet and goodness knows Troy and peace are unmixy things. He seems to have perfected the art of waiting just long enough for us to get into a groove, feeling good and enjoying life, before he has to do his best to drag us back down again.

"He doesn't even pay child support. What the fuck?" I shove my phone in my pocket, and pick up speed, as I make my way back to the Highlander.

When I'm safely inside, I let out a frustrated cry, tossing my phone over to the passenger seat. The further away from me right now, the better.

What is it with people thinking they have a right to force their shit on others?

Why can't they just focus inward—to where the problem *really* is?

You know, take some goddamn personal responsibility and leave everyone else out of it...

"Maybe I'm not cut out for all of this," I whisper, clenching my jaw.

It seems like everywhere I turn, someone is second-guessing me. Home-life, pack-life... Hell, I'm the worst critic.

A strong feeling washes over me and I lean back in my seat. Then, an absurd chuckle escapes my lips as I stare out the window.

"That's it. Screw what others think. I know exactly who I'm going to have as my Beta," I mutter to myself. "And if they don't like it, they can just *suck it*."

CHAPTER 5
SO, THAT'S SETTLED
STONE

S tone could sense the agitation, anxiety, and excitement as it pumped through the bond that had grown between Ella and himself. The sensation was unusual, to be sure. Even when he was Doug's Beta, he had never felt as connected to his brother-in-law as he was becoming to her. At times, it was intense.

The feeling made him extremely uneasy, and oddly enough, incredibly hyped. It was like skydiving, he supposed. While it scared the hell out of a person, it was exhilarating, too.

Beyond that, he wouldn't have been able to explain it if he tried.

The only one who knew how strong the connection was becoming was Clementine, but that was only because she was annoyingly interested in poking her nose where it didn't belong.

But how could he deny her? He knew she was only doing it to keep her mind off of what she'd lost. She was too strong to dwell on it.

All of that didn't negate the fact that Doug had been her fated mate. He'd been everything to her and their time together was cut far too short, even if they did get nearly a century together.

Stone also knew that while she hadn't agreed with Doug's decision to push him out of the pack, she trusted her husband.

He could respect that.

In fact, he was pretty sure Doug had brought Silas in close in an attempt at keeping the peace, but he'd never know for sure. Silas was already causing dissension and by placating him, Doug could keep a close eye on him. Unfortunately for all of them, things hadn't worked the way his brother-in-law had hoped.

Now, it was up to Ella to carry the torch and establish a baseline for peace.

If anyone could do it, he knew she could.

Stone had already seen her grapple with issues that would have made others buckle. Hell, the way in which she accepted her fate as a wolf still boggled his mind.

Yet, here they were...

They were all being called to the Sacred Grove so she could establish the leadership of the pack. She'd chosen her Beta and now she was ready to make it official. She'd even broadcast her intention to the pack all on her own—no help needed from him. Or anyone else, for that matter.

He had to admit, she was a natural.

If he hadn't known any better, he would have thought she was born this way.

Stone was even impressed at how quickly she had learned to lock down her thoughts. As early as last week, she was still having trouble keeping them to herself.

He could tell when she was upset, needing some time away from the kids, or ruminating about him...

But today, he was only able to get snippets of her intentions and they didn't clue him in on the direction she would go. He only sensed he was wrapped up in the decision somewhere.

Part of him wanted desperately to be re-established as Beta. He'd be lying to himself if he didn't accept and admit that. But another part actually hoped he was allowed to remain free. At least, in the broader sense of the term.

He could see things better when he wasn't so close to the action.

Being outside actually helped him keep a better pulse on the pack. Even more so than when he was part of the leadership. He figured he would be more beneficial to Ella that way.

As it was, he felt too close to the situation. This growing need for her was something he'd never expected, but God knew he reveled in the way it felt.

The night she embraced her role as Alpha, he'd promised himself that he'd keep a safe distance—not allowing himself the pleasure of being in her arms or her bed. At least, not until he could be sure what it would mean for them.

If they *were fated,* sex could complicate everything. He feared he'd accidentally claim her before she had a choice in the matter. The last thing he wanted was to remove that choice for her.

She needed to know what she was getting into before they...

He shuddered away from the memory of the other night and the sensations that rolled through his body.

They had been so close—*too close* the other night.

Had the kids not returned when they did, he would have bedded her without a second thought. *To hell with the consequences.*

While the interruption wasn't ideal, it certainly helped more level heads prevail, so to speak.

Stone snickered at the innuendo as he entered the forest. He hadn't bothered shifting into his wolf form. Instead, he wanted to remain centered in himself for now, without amplifying any of his thoughts and desires to the rest of the pack.

He had a feeling Ella wouldn't be in wolf form, anyway. She still wasn't comfortable with shifting back and forth.

That suited him just fine. He wouldn't have to stow clothes or ditch the ones he already wore.

Besides, he was early and he figured it was best to arrive when everyone else did. There'd be less speculation that way. Too many tongues were already wagging about Stone's connection to Ella.

Until he knew what was going on for himself, he didn't need any of them getting in the way.

By the time he came upon the stone circle, half of the pack had already arrived. They were a mixed bunch—half in wolf form and half still human.

When Stone's gaze landed on Ella, the electric current he'd begun to associate with her zipped through his midsection. She was dressed in a flattering button-up top the color of the morning sky and a pair of ripped-up jeans. Her brown hair was a wild mess, but he loved that about her.

"Hey," she breathed when she saw him. Relief filtered through their connection and she visibly relaxed.

"Hey." He walked up to her and gave her hand a squeeze. "Ready for this?"

"To finally have the incessant voices in my head stop questioning me?" she asked, quirking an eyebrow. "Oh, yeah. Wild horses couldn't stop me."

Stone grinned at her enthusiasm. She was happy with her decision. It was clear in the way she held herself. So naturally, he was insanely curious about which direction she was about to go.

He glanced around the circle. More of the pack arrived by the minute.

"You've got a good turnout," he said, leaning in close to her.

"If you can hear their thoughts as loud as I can, you know this is literally the only thing they've cared about for two weeks straight. I'm not surprised they're all coming," she chuckled. "It's like when Asher wanted to get a new phone a year ago. He bugged me for months and months. When I finally said it was time, I'm pretty sure he would have walked on water to get there if I asked him to."

He nodded in agreement. "Fair enough."

While the pack filed in, Ella dropped his hand to make her rounds. She spoke with a few of the pack members she was already familiar with. She said hello to Seth. Then Marta and Clementine. All of which had remained in human form.

She did stop and communicate with a number of the unfamiliar wolves, as well. However, she kept things short and sweet before returning to where he stood.

Finally, after a few more minutes, she clasped her hands in front of her body, thrust her shoulders back, and smiled. "Thank you all for coming here on such short notice."

A consensus moved through the pack and she nodded.

"As I'm sure you're aware, I've been without a second in command—" She dropped her hands and paced a bit. Then she walked into the middle of the circle. "—a Beta, as you call them. And while I promise you, I'll get to that... I have a question for you first."

Stone glanced down, trying hard not to huff out a laugh. He could see already where this was going.

"We haven't really had a chance to get to know each other. I don't know about you, but I like to know who I'm supposed to take orders from," Ella said as she tucked a strand of hair behind her right ear. "Like, there was this one time I was hired by a publishing house and I didn't even meet my direct boss for a year and a half. It was weird and ridiculously hard to care about what I was doing. That sucks, right?"

Again, a consensus rolled through the pack as they tried to figure out where she was going with all of this.

Stone caught Clementine's gaze and a goofy grin spread across her lips. She knew where this was going, too. Hell, she was probably in on it.

Ella inhaled deeply as she turned on her spot to view each pack member. "I'd like for each of you to come out to my place for a Fourth of July picnic."

A couple of people laughed out loud, while a few others stared back at her in shock. While each of them had human lives, pack life never really meant partying together. At least, not like this. Stone knew it would strike a chord with them—but which one remained yet to be seen.

"It'll be a barbecue-style shindig. There will be brats, burgers, probably beer and soda. It should be a good time," Ella said, beaming. "What do you say?"

"The details will be nailed down later this week," Clementine chimed in. "All we know for certain is there will be fireworks."

Stone shook his head. He knew she'd be in on it somehow.

"That sounds like an awesome idea," Seth said, nodding. "And I'll bring my med kit."

Ella practically snorted. "That might be wise. I was telling Stone that I gotta keep my son Asher from blowing up his hand or something."

All eyes turned to Stone like he was in on the plan.

He raised his hands. "This was all her idea. My wish is her..." His words petered out and he flitted his gaze back to Ella.

A bright crimson bled into her cheeks, somehow making her even more gorgeous to him. If he found out they weren't fated and this was just a normal reaction to having a female Alpha, he was going to be pissed. As it was, the fleeting thought of another male from the pack making a move on her was enough to make him see red.

"A-anyway," Ella said, patting the side of her cheek with her palm. "I'll have everything, but if you want to bring a favorite dish to share or whatever, that would be lovely. Also, it'll be family-friendly, so bring the kiddos. Deal?"

"That could be a lot of people. Is your backyard big enough for that?" asked Marta. She planted a hand on her hip and ran the other through her cropped blond hair.

"RSVP and we'll find out. Push comes to shove, I'll rent a gazebo at the park," Ella announced with a shrug.

Marta nodded in approval. If anyone would know just how unruly this sort of thing could get, it was her. She'd been the pack's longest-standing member—and the one who cared most about the integrity and cohesiveness of them, as well.

Ella nodded, evidently happy with the results. "Great, so that's settled."

She walked back to where Stone stood and he sensed her heartbeat kick up a notch.

"Oh, and I suppose you want to know who I picked as my Beta..." she said flippantly. Her dark eyes flitted around the circle with a faint glow that showcased her multicolored Alpha eyes, despite the fact that she stood before them in her human form. A shadow of a smile flitted through her features and she raised her right arm to point. "Everyone, I'd like you to meet your new Beta."

CHAPTER 6
GIRL TIME
ELLA

I have no doubt my decision is going to stir up the hornet's nest, but it has to be done. From what I can tell, there's only one pack member who cares more about the pack than herself, and because of that, she's getting my nomination.

Power rides my words as I point in her direction. "Marta, welcome to the team."

A wave of energy pulsates from the center of my torso to her and both of us shudder from its intensity. It's like there's a cord of dense, blue energy binding us together. I tilt my head, studying it. In some ways, it reminds me of the sensation I feel between me and Stone. Only, slightly different.

Marta steps forward with wide, golden eyes. "Me?"

My finger is still jabbed in her direction, so I lower it, and quirk an eyebrow. "Seriously?"

An enormous smile breaks across her face and she straightens her shoulders. It's clear her question was a knee-jerk reaction. I might be new to this whole thing, but even I can tell she knows I was dead serious. She just wasn't expecting it.

"This is...*an honor,*" Marta proclaims, her voice strong and proud.

Smiling, I step forward and place a hand on her shoulder. "I couldn't think of a better partner. You love this pack, understand its history in contrast to my newness... I know you'll help me navigate the crazy as it comes."

She nods. "I will, indeed. Thank you."

"Personally, I think you should be where I am. But I know that's not how it works." Smiling at her, I then turn to face Stone. "And Stone, I haven't forgotten about you."

His handsome face twitches slightly between contentment and curiosity, until he says, "What do you mean?"

Butterflies flit around my midsection and I grin. Another surge of power rolls through me as I say, "You, are officially the pack's *Delta*. If anything were to happen to Marta or me—I know you'd take good care of the pack. Plus, let's face it, we need the male side represented."

The blue light snakes from me to Marta, then from Marta to Stone. It's like we're links in a chain and I can't help but wonder if that's where the term *'chain of command'* comes from.

Stone shoots me a lopsided grin and tips his head. "It would be my honor."

"This is highly irregular," a male from the pack says, stepping into the circle.

Marta and I turn to face him, but he shrinks back before I even have to say anything.

"Look, I know this is going to take some getting used to. It could be worse, though. Just be glad you're not in my shoes," I say, pressing my lips tight and planting my hands on my hips. "Or having to deal with Silas as your Alpha. Could you imagine?"

A few chuckles and nods escape those who are still in their human form.

I glance down at my watch. "Shit, I gotta bolt, guys. Sorry to drop the news and run, but I promised Avery I'd take her out for a girl's night. Thanks, every-body—" I say, waving quickly and backing toward the exit. I jab a pointer finger out and cluck my tongue. "And don't forget July Fourth... My place! We'll getcha the deets."

With that, I rush out of the Sacred Grove before anyone has a chance to pin me down. The pack erupts into a sea of questions and conversations. However, both Marta and Stone follow me.

"Ella," Marta begins, "we need to have a leadership meeting. There are things that must be done."

I turn around to catch Stone shooting Marta a look of apprehension.

"Look guys, whatever it is, it can wait until tomorrow—"

"No, it must be done tonight. Now that the leadership is established, it must be bound by blood. If nothing else, we must take the oath tonight," Marta insists. "The rest can wait until another day."

"What does that mean?" I ask, fighting the flashbacks to the moment I became a wolf. I rub my hand over my bicep.

"Should anyone attempt to lay claim to our territory, without the pack hierarchy established, we could easily be broken apart. With the blood oath in place, our leadership is official. It also enhances certain *abilities* between us," Marta says. Her blond hair ruffles in the breeze, but she doesn't even shiver from the coolness of the night.

Again, I eye my watch. We only have forty-five minutes before the movie starts and if I'm late, I'll never hear the end of it. "How long will it take?"

"Typically a half hour or so," Marta says, jabbing her thumb back toward the way we came.

"Dammit," I mutter. My gaze flits to Stone.

Stone rubs a hand along his neck. "Marta's right. The pack will be stronger if we can get this done."

I sigh. "Marta, I appreciate your concern, I do. So please don't take this the wrong way...*but I can't.* I promised Avery and she's already feeling left out and anxious because of everything that's happened."

"I understand, but—"

I swipe a hand through the air between us. "I don't mean for my first official act to be ignoring your advice, Marta. So, how about a compromise? What if I go to the movies and when we're done and back home, I'll call the two of you? You can come to my place and we can do what needs to be done when Avery's ready for bed. Sound good?"

I swap my gaze between them.

Stone shrugs. "Seems fair."

"I mean, let's face it, we've gone this long without even having my decision. I highly doubt a couple more hours will make a difference." I chuckle.

Marta sighs in defeat and drops her head slightly. "As you wish."

A relieved breath escapes my lips. "Thank you. *Both of you.* I'll be in touch as soon as I can."

I shoot a crooked smile to Stone as I run my hand down the side of his arm. Then I give his hand a quick squeeze.

He returns the smile and squeezes my hand back. "Have fun. And be careful."

Spinning on my heel I say, "I'm the epitome of careful."

Then, wouldn't you know it, the gnarly grasp of a fallen branch gets caught in my shoelaces. I stumble for a moment, but thank the stars, manage to stay vertical.

Heat flares to my cheeks as I turn around and give them both the thumbs up. "I'm okay."

Stone snorts under his breath, shaking his head slightly.

Marta just stares at me with what I can only assume is wide-eyed horror.

I heave a breath, roll my eyes at myself, and keep walking with my head held high. Lord help me, if I could just not make a fool of myself around the people I'm trying to impress, that would be great.

Somehow, I doubt that's an accomplishment I can manage.

Glancing at my watch again, I start running and consider shifting into my wolf. But I need my car if we're going to get to the theater together.

As it is, it'll take me fifteen minutes to get home in the Highlander and another ten to get to the theatre. I'll be lucky if Avery isn't already having a full-blown panic attack by the time I get home. She hates getting to the movies too late to enjoy the previews.

Thankfully, the trip home is faster than I antici-pate. When I open the front door, Avery is just exiting the bathroom with her hair pulled into a fresh pony and donning a different outfit than when I left her. Either she wants to look good in case she meets anyone her own age, or she was TikToking for the next few days and needed to change outfits.

Heaven forbid it look like she recorded them all in one go.

"Ready?" I ask, shooting her a cheesy grin.

I'm so glad she can't hear my thoughts the way the pack can because she definitely would have been concerned picking up on my anxiety to be back in time.

Oh, yeah, she totally gets that from her dad...

"Yup," she says, bounding down the stairs.

I nod and tip my chin to holler up the stairs. "We're heading out, Ash. Behave while we're gone. No parties and no burning the house down."

Asher pokes his head out of his doorway. An enormous headset rests over his ears, making him look like a Cyberman from Dr. Who. He pulls it away from his right ear. "What?"

I swipe a hand in the air, shaking my head. "Nevermind. Don't forget to eat. We'll be back later."

"Kay," he mutters, vanishing back into his teen-man cave.

"Bye, Mom. Bye, Avery. Have a wonderful time," I mutter under my breath sarcastically. Then I turn to Avery. "Yeesh, you guys need to get better at goodbyes. Who raised you?"

Avery shrugs.

"Come on," I laugh, looping my right arm through her left. "A night devoid of fart jokes awaits."

She throws her head back. "Thank God."

Once outside, I drop her arm to lock the front door

behind us. Avery continues on to the Highlander, hopping into the front seat before I can even make it to my door.

"Where do you want to eat?" I ask when I get behind the wheel.

"Not sure yet. Let's see how we feel after gorging ourselves with popcorn and sugar," she says grinning at me.

I snicker and put the vehicle in reverse. "Fair point."

When we pull up to the theater, all of the anxiety I was feeling earlier has vanished. In fact, I feel a sense of calm I haven't felt in weeks. It's like the entire pack has breathed a huge, collective sigh of relief. Had I known it was going to be that easy to appease them, I would have picked my Beta right after the fight with Silas.

Granted, there are still a few who are concerned about my choices but they're falling in line. They know the group as a whole has to jive, so they're willing to let their individual opinions subside. I suppose it was no different when Doug was here and they had to deal with Silas. It kinda explains why they were willing to go along with the absurdity of it.

God, I hope I picked better than Doug did.

"Come on, Mom. It starts in five minutes," Avery says, dragging me from the ticket counter to the concession stand. "We need to get the goods and get a seat."

"Relax, woman. There's only one person in front of us. Pretty sure we'll be fine," I say, giving her a squeeze across her shoulders.

The woman in front of us turns around. Her black hair swings in the motion, splaying like a fan. "I thought that was you," she beams.

"*Alanna*, twice in one day? It's like we're on the same wavelength," I say, laughing softly. Maybe our meeting in the coffee shop earlier was fortuitous. Sweeping my hand out, I point at my daughter. "Alanna, this is my mini-me, Avery. Avery, this is Alanna."

Avery tucks her arm close to her body and waves. "Hi."

"What movie are you going to?" Alanna asks, grabbing an enormous popcorn from the tall, red-haired concessions worker. Then she steps aside, so we can place our order.

"Fantastic Beasts. You?" I ask, leaning up to the counter. The red-haired guy stares at me with the kind of boredom only a teen can pull off. "Can we get two large Cherry Cokes, a box of Milk Duds, a bag of Twizzlers, and one of those?" I point at Alanna's giant bag of popcorn.

"Yup," the guy says, barely blinking at the request. He sets to work immediately, grabbing the candy and setting it on the counter. I'm actually impressed when he grabs the right ones.

"I'm going to Fantastic Beasts, too," Alanna says,

surprise flitting through her face. "It's so nice you have someone to go with. It's just me, so..."

"Did you—" I turn to face Avery, trying to gauge if she'll approve of my next few words. Her eyes are planted on the candy counter and it's doubtful she's heard a word either of us have said. She clearly wants something beyond what I ordered. So, to hell with it. "Did you want to sit with us?"

"Are you sure? I don't want to intrude—" Alanna says, shifting her gaze to my daughter.

"Mom, can I get the Snowcaps, too?" Avery asks, clearly not fussed.

I nod. "If you can get his attention, go for it."

She pushes her way past me, evidently a girl on a mission. I take a step back to give her more room.

"Well, I think Avery will be fine with it. And I'd hate for you to sit alone," I say, reaching for the popcorn being extended in my direction.

I no sooner say the words and a strange sensation creeps down my spine. It's like someone poured cold water down my back as icy tendrils spread out. It reminds me of the way I felt when the guy chastised me earlier for who I was hanging out with.

Shivering, I glance around the movie theater entry. People are mulling around—some exiting, some playing arcade games, and some lining up for their movies. None of them overtly make me think they're giving off the vibes I'm feeling.

"Are you okay?" Alanna asks, her expression turning dark.

Slowly, I return my gaze to her. "Yeah, I...*think* so."

However, I'm not entirely sure if my words ring true.

Something is not right and I can't put my finger on what it is.

CHAPTER 7
A LITTLE LATE FOR THAT

ELLA

Avery hands me my soda and I take it, only halfway paying attention. Instead, my instincts are on some kind of hyper-alert and I can't seem to shake it.

Alanna's expression hasn't changed. She continues to watch me with intense interest.

"Come on, guys. We'll miss the movie," I say, blinking away the sensation so I can lead the way.

Whatever this is, it's not going away, and I'll be damned if I let it ruin my girl's night with Avery.

I hand over my ticket to the kid acting as the gate-keeper and he points in the direction of the theater where our show is playing. Alanna and Avery do the same and before I know it, we're in our seats. I'm the one designated to the middle, as Alanna takes up the spot to my left and Avery to my right, which suits me just fine. When I have both kids, it's where I'm seated, too.

"So, have you read the books?" Alanna asks, arching around me to view Avery.

It's nice of her to reach out to my daughter instead of focusing just on me.

Avery takes a bite of her Twizzler before nodding. "All of 'em. You?"

"Same," Alanna grins. She turns to face me with a curious stare.

I raise my hands to the ceiling. "Who do you think taught her to read?"

Again Alanna smiles, nodding in approval. She settles back into her seat just as the lights begin to dim.

As hard as I try to relax and enjoy the previews, the agitated feeling doesn't subside. If anything, it grows stronger, and I'm on the verge of calling on Marta and Stone to see if they're sensing anything out of the ordinary.

However, Stone beats me to the punch. His agitation hits me before his words invade my mind.

Ella, are you okay?

I inhale a sharp breath. *I'm fine. What's going on?*

Something's not right. Where are you? His words, while inside my mind, have an edge of uneasiness clinging to them.

The movie theater. I fire back.

Stay put. Marta and I are on our way.

With that, his connection to me vanishes and I'm left feeling like a huge hole opened up in my midsection. If Stone's feeling *whatever this is*, then it's more than just my normal anxiety. It's tied to my new werewolf senses.

While that should make me feel better, you know, because they're working the way they should be, the fact that something is amiss does quite the opposite.

I draw in a deep breath through my nose and try to focus on the screen.

Alanna nudges me with her shoulder. "What's going on with you?"

I shoot her a sideways glance. She's not a part of the pack, so there's no way I'm going to freak her out with the crazy that is my new life.

"Nothing. Just feeling kinda off," I say, trying to smile as sincerely as possible. "It's been a weird day."

She eyes me for a moment before nodding sharply and returning her gaze to the movie.

I glance over to Avery, who thankfully, appears to be oblivious to her mother's plight.

Teenager attention span for the win.

I'd hate for her to realize the wolf stuff is invading into our time together—*yet again*. She's been so patient with me, but it's also no secret she's not a fan of this new change to the dynamic.

Hell, I'm still not a hundred percent sure how I feel about it.

As the movie drags on, I can't say I've paid attention to any of it.

The pack is mobilizing and moving in our direction.

Plus, Stone's energy is heightened in a way I haven't felt from him before. He's agitated and oddly enough, on the verge of indignation.

It's not like him.

To add insult to injury, the theater seats are like rocks and my ass is going numb. I'm literally counting down the minutes until the show is over and I can stretch my legs.

"Mom, are you gonna eat any more of that?" Avery asks, pointing at my lap.

I glance down, surprised to find a half-eaten bag of popcorn resting there.

No clue how that happened.

Shaking my head, I hand it over to her. "You know, I gotta run to the bathroom. I'll be right back."

I get up slowly, letting the blood rush from my backside to my hamstrings. I groan, then edge my way out of our row of seats.

When I exit the theater, I exhale the breath I didn't realize had been clinging to my lungs. Getting up and moving around does me some good, and my energy settles a bit.

I make my way down the enormous hallway with movie posters plastered everywhere and side shoots that lead off to other movies being played. When I reach the bathroom, I head straight into a stall to do my business on autopilot.

My mind is cycling through what's happening beyond these walls and I wish I knew what the cause of all the agitation was. Hopefully, it will be answered soon, since the pack is closing in.

I walk over to the sink, thrust my hand under the soap dispenser, and plunge my hands into the tepid water.

The bathroom door flies open and a woman the size of Fort Knox enters. Instantly, the hairs all over my body stand on end and my back stiffens, despite myself. I have no idea who she is, but something about her tells me she's no friend.

In fact, she smells like a wolf, but she's definitely not from Black Crater. Instead, her scent reminds me more of the mountains.

Or maybe it's just her size.

She narrows her eyes at me, then a slow, menacing grin spreads across her features.

My heart thumps in my chest as I scramble for what my next move should be.

Ella, there's another pack moving into our territory. That's what we've been feeling. Stay alert, and please, be careful. We'll be there soon. Stone communicates through our mental link.

A little late for that.

I stare at the woman in the bathroom. Her cropped purple hair and dark black eyeliner make her look like she should be in a biker gang and not a werewolf pack.

Despite myself, I snicker.

Look at me, making assumptions about what is or isn't like a werewolf.

Pot and kettle.

"What are you laughing at, little Alpha?" the woman sneers, edging closer.

"Oh, nothing," I mutter, shaking my head. "You wouldn't get it."

Emo chick narrows her eyes and growls—*like actually growls*—at me.

"Don't you know it's not polite to bare your teeth in public?" I spit back before I can think of something better.

The woman lunges forward, her hands extended out for my throat. While I might not be the mountain of muscle she is, I can still be fast when I actually see danger coming at me. I dodge her attempt at the last second and she hits the wall. The momentary win doesn't last long, since she spins right back around, ready for another attempt.

I rear up, planting my foot in her midsection and thrusting her back. She slams into the counter.

Suddenly, the door opens and Avery enters the bathroom. Her expression goes from normal to freaked in a matter of microseconds.

I thrust a hand out, pointing to the door. "Avery —*out.*"

Unfortunately, she inherited her F-response from me. So, of course, she freezes.

"Out," I repeat, putting some power into the command.

The woman beside me shudders in response, and my daughter cries out, running from the bathroom.

In an instant, the woman beside me rushes out after her, but not for the same reason. Her intent was clear from the smirk on her face. She's going after her.

"Shit," I spit, following after the two of them.

When I hit the hallway, I sputter to a stop. The concessions area is filled with other wolves—mostly women by the looks of it.

But standing in the center is one man.

He's gotta be at least six foot five and has enough muscle on him that I'd hate to have to go toe-to-toe with him. Add on top, it's obvious he's groomed to be intimidating. His freshly shaved bald head shines under the flashing theater lighting, which is saying something because his skin is incredibly dark. His goatee twitches as he smirks at me.

Whoever this group is, he's their Alpha.

Despite never being taught how to sense it, the power rolls off of him and feels similar to my own.

My eyes flit around the space, landing on Avery, who's in the clutches of the woman from the bathroom. With absolutely no fight in her, she stands there with a pale face and wild eyes.

If I don't do something quickly, it's going to take me weeks to get her back to normal.

"Let her go," I say slowly, a strange sort of calm settling over me.

These people—*wolves*—don't know me from Jack, but so help me, if they mess with my kid, they'll live to regret it.

The Alpha steps forward, his arms spread out wide, and palms raised to the ceiling. "Is that any way to welcome us?"

"Who said you were welcome?" I fire back, crossing my arms over my chest.

A hearty, boisterous laugh erupts from his lips. It's the kind of laugh that could actually make you giggle under better circumstances.

"I like her. She's got spunk," he says, jabbing a pointer finger toward me, and glancing at the women around him. "Don't you like her?"

A commotion breaks out as they glance at each other.

"That's not all I've got," I spit through gritted teeth.

I flick my gaze back to Avery, trying to relay with my eyes that I'll get her out of this.

The other Alpha quirks an eyebrow. "Is that so? What else have you got, little one? Go on."

"Keep holding my daughter against her will and you'll find out," I say, and despite myself, a growl rides my words.

Power rises through my midsection until I feel like I'm about to float because of it. The urge to shift is strong, but I refuse to be the first to make that kind of move.

Especially in a place so openly...*human.*

The last thing I needed to do is freak out the community at large.

He tsks. "Now, now... Is that any way to treat us?"

I narrow my gaze. "No offense, but I don't know you. So, you can kindly *fuck off.*"

"Big words for an Alpha all by her lonesome," purple-hair chides, chuckling darkly under her breath, and glancing around at her pack mates.

I flash my gaze to her and for the briefest of moments, she flinches.

"Mom," Avery cries, tears brimming in her eyes. Her lip quivers and it's enough to throw me over the edge.

I inhale sharply and lock my eyes on the one with her hands wrapped around my kid's arms.

"I won't repeat myself," I say, feeling the power in me rise. When I speak the next words, I unleash the intensity of it straight at her. *"Let her go."*

The power of it erupts from the center of my body, flowing along the current of my words. Half of the pack behind their Alpha stumble a step or two back. The woman with the purple hair does as I ask, releasing my daughter just long enough for her to worm her way out of her vicinity.

Avery rushes forward, slamming into me, and wrapping her arms around my waist. I pull her into me, draping my right arm protectively around her, and shifting her slightly behind me.

A huge smirk slides across the Alpha's face.

I don't need to be part of his pack to know that he's getting off on being near another female with power. He clearly surrounds himself with them.

Fuck.

I really should have taken Marta up on that whole blood bond thing.

Things are about to get messy.

CHAPTER 8
SETTING PRECEDENT
STONE

Ella's emotions were fluctuating between panic and indignation and with every swing of the pendulum, it pushed Stone further to the edge.

If anyone hurt her... He wouldn't be held responsible for the destruction that would be left in his wake.

The intensity of that belief—and the fact that it had lodged itself deeply into the core of his very being—surprised even him. He'd never been one to get too hung up on the judgment or justice of others when it didn't particularly impact him.

And while Ella was the pack's Alpha, which meant whatever happened to her *would* affect him, he would be kidding himself if he didn't admit it was more than that. Of course, it was.

Just *how much more* had yet to be discerned.

However, the fact remained, he was willing to do

whatever was necessary, should he arrive and find Ella or her daughter hurt.

He shuddered away the thought.

Ella could handle herself. He'd witnessed it.

But this was a brand new kind of threat. With Silas, it was her against a select few.

She'd never been up against any of the other packs before and if preliminary intel was right, the pack who'd ventured into Black Crater was a formidable one. Should they decide to make a move, Stone wasn't sure if they'd be able to stop them.

Philip Reinhardt and his Portland Pack members were not to be trifled with. They had maintained their status as one of the largest neighboring packs for the past two hundred or so years. They knew how to stand on their own and only moved when they wanted something.

Or more specifically, *someone.*

Stone knew all too well that Philip had a thing for strong females. His pack was almost exclusively compromised of them.

The moment he got a whiff of Ella's power, he'd want to incorporate her into his fold. Hell, he'd probably want to mate her and—

A growl erupted from the middle of Stone's chest.

Over his dead fucking body.

He pushed himself into a run, then shifted in midair. To hell with his clothes—or anything else, for that matter. He had to get to Ella as quickly as he could.

Marta joined him somewhere along the way, though Stone barely even registered her at first. She, too, was in her wolf form, as they raced along the wooded areas behind the town.

Within a few minutes, they would be at the theater. He could sense a plan formulating within Ella, but he couldn't understand what it was—or what she was expecting of them.

Now was not a great time to learn how to mask her thoughts.

What is Ella up to? Can you tell? Stone asked, communicating through the pack link to Marta.

If anyone would know, it would be her Beta first.

No—without the blood bond, I only get a vague sense of her emotions. She's formulating something, but she's not broadcasting her plan directly to me. Has she to you? Marta asked. Her gaze was locked on the path ahead, but the agitation that rolled off of her mirrored his own.

No. It's the same for me.

Additional pack members joined them from the woods beyond, each of them asking the same questions of Marta and Stone that they had been asking of themselves. It appeared, Ella hadn't broadcast any of her intentions to the rest of them. They only knew something was terribly wrong and she needed support.

It was a terrible way to go into a fight.

If they made it through this, Stone realized he and Marta would need to step up and help Ella understand the hierarchy and dynamics that interconnects everything. That way, she could support the pack, and in turn, they could support her. Everyone needed a game plan in order to be most effective and that came from the top down.

In theory, he was sure Ella was aware of this, but with everything she'd had dumped into her lap, she was operating from survival. And from what he gathered, she wasn't used to surviving by leaning on others.

It didn't help that Stone thought there would have been more time to get her up to speed before anything this dire arose.

Fucking Murphy's Law.

By the time he and Marta arrived at the theater, their grouping was at least twenty members strong, with more on the way. Stone prayed that would be enough to take down an attack from the Portland Pack, but he doubted it. They were a formidable group and the Black Crater Pack was a disorganized mess at present.

Marta, Stone—get everyone ready. I'm sweet-talking the Alpha and trying to get him outside.

Ella's command hit Stone with a force that compelled him to stop dead in his tracks. Beside him,

Marta did the same. Neither of them had expected the intensity of it.

Are you okay? How's Avery? Stone responded.

We're fine. I may need you and Marta to take down the woman with the purple hair and the two that will be standing beside their Alpha. They seem to be the next in charge. Keep them, and everyone else, at bay so I can focus on the Alpha directly. Get the others ready to move. She commanded.

How many are in there with you? Marta interjected as she paced back and forth.

A surge of pride swelled inside Stone. Despite the lack of a blood bond, and barely any direction, the communication link between the three of them was growing stronger with each thought that passed through them.

Only thirteen, as far as I can tell.

Good, we are greater in numbers. Marta replied.

Stone could tell this bit of news had Marta hopeful that they might still have an advantage yet. He, on the other hand, fought back any thoughts of optimism. For all they knew, there were more pack members outside the theater. And even if there weren't, they still had plenty of work to do. He didn't want to derail it by being blindsided.

He might be a part of the pack again, but he had been an outcast too long to let that part of him go.

Stone, you take the one with the purple hair. I've got the other two, I know exactly who they will be. Marta said.

An excited, anticipatory energy rolled off Marta and Stone wasn't sure if it was because of what came next, or the fact that she was elevated to Beta.

He relayed his agreement and a plan began to take shape. While the Portland Pack would know more wolves were inbound, they wouldn't be able to gauge the actual number. That meant, if they played their cards right, they could make the Portland Pack believe they held the advantage. Maybe make them think the pack numbers had dwindled drastically because of Ella.

Then, they could turn the tables.

He and Marta tossed the concept back and forth until they could come to an agreement on how to proceed. Their plan wasn't perfect, but it might be enough that when they showed their sign of strength and solidarity, the Portland Pack would be taken aback.

Especially considering Ella's newness to this world.

By the time the theater came into view, Ella's agitation had waned. It was replaced by something else—something Stone couldn't quite put his finger on. He took it as a sign to approach delicately.

Marta and Stone slowed, circling the building until the parking lot was in view.

Ella and her daughter were huddled together, with the Portland Pack gathered in a semi-circle around them.

As Ella described, there were thirteen of them within view. Every single one of them was still in their human form, which surprised Stone. Ordinarily, a pack with as much power and recognition as they had would have made their presence known in their wolf form. It was easier to show dominance that way.

Do you sense any others hidden in the shadows? Stone projected to Marta. His gaze swept the shadows, seeking anything that might be out of the ordinary.

None. It appears to be a scouting party. Marta said, edging up until she was shoulder to shoulder with him.

Why would Philip bother to join a scouting party? Stone asked before he thought better of it.

Of course, he already knew why. News of Ella must have traveled to him and he came to see her for himself.

Marta must have sensed his recognition because she didn't bother answering.

What would you like us to do? Seth's question tumbled at Stone, but he knew it was meant for everyone.

Hold back. I think I have this under control. Ella responded.

Spread out, just in case. Enclose the theater in a circle so there are no surprises. Marta interjected, stepping away from Stone to get a better vantage point.

The rest of the pack fanned out, doing as Marta

asked. Each of them waited in the darkness, ready for any shift in plans.

Ella's energy was certainly more relaxed, however, Stone couldn't help but feel as though something was still off. He couldn't understand how things could have ended diplomatically so soon.

It didn't feel right.

They're leaving. Evidently, they wanted to be the first to congratulate me on my new role. Ella communicated through the pack link. *Though, I gotta admit they have a shitty way of saying hello.*

Are you certain? Marta responded. *They are leaving?*

I am. Ella confirmed.

He couldn't say he was relieved, per se, but Stone had to admit it was better that none of them had to fight. Particularly since Ella's daughter was in the mix and she looked anything but happy.

Avery was huddled up beside her mother with her arms wrapped tightly around Ella's waist. While she tried to hide her face with her hair, it was evident from where Stone stood that she had been crying.

An intense wave of anger tightened Stone's chest and a low rumble escaped his throat.

That child wasn't a part of this world, and for Philip to intercept Ella the way he had, it didn't sit well with Stone. He would have thought they'd have more decorum than that. Instead, this felt deliberate. Like they were making a point of showcasing Ella's biggest weaknesses.

Fuck. He was setting precedent—and maybe even shooting a warning shot.

This was all for show.

Despite himself, Stone padded his way to Ella from the shadows beyond the parking lot.

Where are you going? Marta asked as surprise flooded through the link.

He walked between the cars until he came up behind the Portland Pack. Without responding to Marta, he pushed his way through the first few until they began to part for him.

When Ella caught sight of him, a wave of relief and joy overcame him, and he took up his place at her side. She rested her hand on the top of his head, rubbing between his ears.

He'd never thought anything of a human's touch when he was in wolf form before, but he could certainly get used to hers.

"And who is this?" Philip asked. He crossed his arms over his body and jabbed an index finger toward Stone.

One of the women behind him stepped up and whispered into his ear.

"Stone Lachlan? Well, now, isn't that interesting?" Philip said with a smirk. "Last I'd heard, you had been outcast."

"Things change," Ella said defiantly.

Stone surged with pride as he sat there. His gaze flitted from person to person, cataloging each and every face until he was sure he would be able to spot them on sight and not only by sense.

"Well, Ella, it was lovely to meet you," Philip said. He stepped forward, reaching out, and kissing her hand. He lingered there for a moment, gazing deeply into her eyes. "We'll be watching you *with great interest.*"

Oh goody. As she took her hand back, Ella's thought broadcast loud and clear. Whether she meant to or not was questionable.

Stone, on the other hand, had a sudden urge to rip Philip limb from limb.

CHAPTER 9
CHAOS ENSUES

ELLA

How the hell did I ever find this work fascinating?

The cursor taunts me, blinking in anticipation of whatever fascinating insight I'm about to write regarding an experimental erectile dysfunction drug—only the insight doesn't come. Instead, any thoughts housed in my brain flee, leaving me empty.

I bite the side of my lip and drum my fingertips across my desk.

Something that feels suspiciously like panic claws at my ribcage. It's like a bird has been trapped and is thumping around in an attempt to escape.

Writing about medications and how they help or hinder people used to seem like an important job. It let me balance my desire to write with my love of research and health topics.

But now...

After everything that's happened, I'm not sure I can go back to a job that feels so mundane and...*ordinary*. Everything about it feels in direct conflict with what I've now become.

I mean, I'm Alpha for a werewolf pack, for crying out loud.

I'm freakin' *supernatural*.

If last night's run-in with the Portland Pack didn't hit that home, I don't know what else will.

While we were able to come to an agreement, their Alpha was way too touchy-feely. Plus, I got the sneaky suspicion he has a hidden agenda. Stone seemed to think so, too.

I bet werewolves don't get erectile dysfunction.

The thought barrels at me before I have a chance to filter it.

Snickering under my breath, I shake it away. But, of course, my mind meanders to Stone. He certainly doesn't have that problem, either.

I sigh, grinning contently, as I sink back in my seat.

It's been a few days since our close call and yet, the way he felt, and the way my body reacted still plays on my mind. Whenever he's nearby, I lose all sense of myself, and I want nothing more than to be a teenager again—throwing caution to the wind and doing unspeakable things with him.

I'm not even sure I'd regret it.

I push myself away from my desk and stand up to

stretch. The words aren't coming and I know better than to push myself when I'm not feeling it. If I did, things will come out snarky or contrite. Not a good combination for those poor guys who are, in fact, suffering.

As it is, my boss is already getting restless with me.

He was empathetic during the divorce. He was understanding when I said I was moving. Now that everything is settled, though, it's clear he wants me to get back to my full-time gig. The last thing I need is to send him a crappy article for my first assignment back.

Why erectile dysfunction?

Rolling my head from side to side, the urge to run filters into my awareness. It's not just because this article makes me want to hurl myself off a bridge, either.

It's a wolf thing—and so weird that it's a thing now.

However, it makes sense. We're not far off from the next full moon and I haven't given much credence to my wolf. Hell, I haven't even shifted since the fight with Silas.

If I'm honest, it kinda scares me to give in too much to it.

I push in my chair and make my way over to my dresser. In some ways, working from my bedroom actually comes in handy. But I'm not gonna lie... I'm looking forward to the day when I can convert one of the kids' bedrooms into an office.

Screw being one of those parents that keeps their kid's bedroom for them exactly as it was when they left. It's my forever home, dammit. It's not like either of them will have a "mom room."

Sure, they'll always have a place to crash, but they'll have a couch or a guest room to come home to.

I get dressed quickly, excited to get out of the house for a few minutes. Thankfully, my running pants have a hip pocket, so I grab my phone from my desk and slide it inside. Running is now a much more pleasant experience, that's for sure.

When I leave my bedroom, I head straight for the upstairs bathroom to grab a ponytail holder and get my hair up and out of my face.

"Guys, I'm going for a run," I call out, as I loop the band around my hair.

"Mkay," is the grunt of acknowledgment that greets me.

I'm not sure which kid said it. Maybe it was both.

Clearly, my weird behavior no longer fazes them.

I shake my head and continue past their doorways with a wave. They both wave back, barely looking up from their devices.

The jaunt down the stairs is fast and before I know it, I've hit the great outdoors. Inhaling deeply the fragrance of freshly cut grass, flowers, and afternoon sunshine, I can't help but smile as my spirits lift.

By the time I hit the trail, my blood is crying out to run—run fast, run far. *Shift.*

I pick up speed, letting my muscles stretch with the effort as I take in long gulps of air. It's so weird, I can practically feel the extra oxygen coursing through my body and my muscles growing in the exertion.

Suffice it to say, this run is much more pleasant than my first one. With my phone secured in my workout pants and my sweat-wicking shirt and bra in place, it's downright euphoric.

Granted, it helps that I understand this urge to run now, too.

I continue down the trail in the direction of the lakeside park with the intention of hitting the bathroom and turning back around. No need to go crazy and run beyond that point.

The trail is buzzing with people this afternoon. Evidently, early evening is a more popular time than late morning for the crowds to come out. There are people running, walking, and biking everywhere I look. In fact, I haven't seen a single trailside bench that wasn't occupied.

The guy on the bench closest to me wipes frantically at the coffee spilled over his dress shirt. He has an air of importance, so I can only imagine how he must be feeling. I pretend to not notice and keep on running.

Smiling to myself, I enjoy the atmosphere as I get closer to the park. So far, thankfully, tiny mom bladder hasn't struck—but it's only a matter of time.

Up ahead, I notice a woman with blazing red hair —the kind of red that only comes in a vibrant-color dye box. She's walking slowly, limping along with a cane in her right hand.

My heart squishes for her. It must be hard to get out to be mobile, but there she is, making it happen.

Good for her.

Heading toward me is another woman with a purse clutched to her body, as if she's expecting someone to jump out at any moment and snatch it from her. Her blond hair is pulled in a tight bun and I briefly wonder if her knickers are in a twist, too.

She gives the red-haired woman a side-eyed glance and a sneer flits its way to her face. Before I have time to be annoyed with her, the purse strap on her bag snaps and she nearly drops her goods. She fumbles with it, doing a rendition of a ballet piece as she tries to maintain her contact with it.

Pressing my lips tight, I snicker under my breath at the ironic justice playing out in front of me.

By the time I run by, she has a grip on her purse and a disgruntled expression on her face.

I wave as I go past but her face is pinched too tightly to tell if she notices.

Within a minute, I catch up to the woman walking with a cane.

I open my mouth to tell her I'm passing on her left, so he doesn't freak out, but before the words can spring from my mouth, my right foot catches on the back of my left and I go down. Luckily, I point myself toward the grass and end up doing an ungraceful tuck-and-roll, narrowly missing some decorative bushes.

I come to a stop, sprawled out flat on my back, staring up at the tree branches and blue sky overhead.

So much for my werewolf reflexes getting any better. If anything, they've gotten worse.

"You okay there?" the woman asks standing over me. Her red hair is like an intense sunset flapping in the breeze as she plants her cane on the ground beside me. Then, she reaches out for my hand. Her inquisitive green eyes give me a good once over while she waits for me to catch my breath and reengage my brain.

Shaking away the dizziness, I nod and extend my hand to her, accepting her offering. I do my best to rise on my own accord, so I don't pull her off balance, too. That would be just my luck.

"Thanks. Yeah, I don't know what happened. One minute I was upright, feeling good. The next I was tumbling ass over tits."

She chuckles, her face brightening. "That's such a colorful way to put it."

"It was how I pictured it in my head." I laugh with a shrug. "Good lord, you'd think after forty-two years, I'd know how to put one foot in front of the other without face-planting." I extend a hand. "I'm Ella, by the way."

"June," she says with a nod, "but everyone calls me Jinx."

"That's a cool nickname. How'd you get it?" I ask,

brushing off my backside and plucking some grass from my hair.

"Well, you might not believe it, but chaos seems to follow me wherever I go." She grins.

"You know, funnily enough, I could see that."

Again, she laughs. "Are you new here? I don't think I've seen you before."

"Yeah, we moved to Black Crater a month ago," I say, nodding. "How long have you been here?"

She blows out a puff of air. "Longer than I care to admit."

"So, your whole life, then?" I ask, quirking an eyebrow.

"Something like that." She turns her attention to a kid blazing down the trail on a mint green foot-powered scooter. He couldn't be more than eight years old. As he gets closer, she steps off the path and onto the grass with me.

"Well, there are definitely worst places to stick around. I plan to grow old and die here," I admit.

Her lips twitch into a smile.

The kid on the scooter passes us, oblivious to the world around him.

Suddenly, the back wheel on his scooter pops off, spinning itself into the bushes nearby. The back end slams onto the concrete with a screech and he nearly tumbles over the handles.

My hands fly to my mouth. "Oh my gosh—"

Rushing over, I help the kid right himself. "Are you okay?"

He turns to me with wide blue eyes but doesn't say a word. A man rushes up behind him on a bike. "Adam, you okay?"

I smile at him and back away. Dad to the rescue is obviously better than a strange woman in the face.

Turning back to June, I can't help but shake my head. "Wow, you weren't kidding. Jinx is a very fitting name."

Her cheeks blaze as she nods in agreement. "It does seem to follow me around."

"Well, it was nice to meet you. However, I now feel my *mom bladder* calling and need to make it to the restroom before anything else goes awry." I point toward the park.

"Nice to meet you, too, Ella. Maybe I'll catch you around again sometime," she says, with a quick wave. "Stay vertical, if you can." There's a mischievous twinkle in her eyes before she turns and continues slowly on her way.

"Thanks," I mumble, scratching at the top of my head. My fingertips bump into something hard and I pull a small twig from my hair. Rolling my eyes, I flick it to the ground.

As I turn around to resume my sprint to the bathroom, I sense one of the pack members closing in fast. My gaze floats the spaces nearby and it lands on Seth as he jogs toward me. He's not in his EMT garb today, but instead, dressed in jogging shorts and a bright cyan tank top that shows off his dark muscles.

Sighing in relief, I wave.

"Hey, Seth it's nice to see—" I begin.

"Hey Ella. I couldn't help but notice your tumble," he says. "And, uh, I know you mean well, but you really need to be careful who you get close to," Seth says, cutting me off with a grimace. He glances over his shoulder giving June a once-over.

"Oh, come on. Not you, too. This is ridiculous. What is it with werewolves thinking we can't be friendly with people outside the pack?" I lament, running my fingertips over my right eyebrow to stop it from twitching.

"It's not that. It's just..." his voice trails off and his gaze falls to the ground. "You know, it's not really my place to question you. But you might want to chat with Marta. She'll be able to explain things better. I just don't want you falling in with the wrong sorts." He shoots me a look of apology, then pats the side of my arm. "Nice to see you out and about, though."

Without another word, he stalks off.

My mouth pops open and I stare at his retreating back.

Over the past few weeks, I've gotten to know Seth pretty well. I would never have expected him to be this way. If anything, I would have thought he'd be all for diversity.

What is it with people lately?

CHAPTER 10

BLOOD BOND

ELLA

"Are you sure this is necessary?" I ask, frowning at the shiny ritual blade being offered to me. Daylight is waning and my backyard fire pit behind Marta is more pronounced as one of the pack members drops another log on the fire and stokes it.

Only a few of them came over to witness this blood bond thing, but it's enough to make me nervous. Especially since the only ones I really know are Seth and Clementine.

I stare up into Marta's expectant gaze and she thrusts the knife in my direction again in response.

I take it from her. "Shit."

I can think of plenty of other things I'd rather be doing right now. Like listening to the kids fight. Having a contentious call with the ex. Hell, even writing my erectile dysfunction article ranks higher.

Why did I have to pick a Beta who was a stickler for the rules?

Dumb.

"It won't be as bad as you think," Stone offers, his emerald eyes glinting in the dying light. He's dressed in a pair of khaki summer shorts and a loose-fitting white t-shirt. Both of which give him an easy-going vibe. You'd never know he was about to drink blood like he was a vampire, not a werewolf.

I make a face. "Easy for you to say."

He nods. "It is. I've had to do it before. Remember?"

"Oh, right," I say, turning the blade over in my hand. I hadn't thought about his past Beta initiation, what with all the panic wreaking havoc in my brain.

"Once we are bonded, your healing abilities will accelerate, if that's what you're worried about. The wound will heal within minutes," Marta says dismissively. She's also got a relaxed vibe going on tonight, with a floaty kind of sundress and sandals on. Her blond hair has taken on a glowing golden tint in the firelight, catching my attention.

The two of them look far more put together than my frumpy t-shirt and capris look.

"Marta's right," Stone says, nodding. "You'll have access to everything our lineages have brought into the mix."

I shake my head. "No, it's not that. I'm just a baby,

and more worried about the initial pain, but thank you."

"That is insignificant," Marta says with the swipe of her hand.

My eyes widen. "Yippee."

Stone chuckles. "Let's just get this over with and you'll see. The lead-up is far worse than actually doing it. It's like going in for a vaccine. Once it's over, you wonder what you were ever worried about."

"Ella, this will empower the pack as a whole. It's vitally important we forge our connection and establish our leadership. We don't need another experience like last night," Marta says pointedly. "As it is, the Portland Pack hasn't left town just yet and it's putting me on edge. If another..."

I grind my teeth together.

She's right, I know she is.

But this just seems so...*barbaric*.

"All right, let's do this. But for the love of all that's holy, talk about something fun to keep my mind off of this craziness," I say, shooting them both my *mom glare*.

My gaze extends over Marta's shoulder, and I grin half-heartedly at the other pack members who are hanging out in my backyard.

From beside the fire, Albert, a guy with a thick neck and long brown hair that he's pulled into a haphazard ponytail, raises his beer bottle in salute from an Adirondack chair.

Clementine clasps her hands together, steepling her fingertips beneath her chin as she leans forward in her chair. Seth, on the other hand, looks as apprehensive as I feel as he stands up straighter and watches with wide, expectant eyes.

"It's just a little prick of the finger, Ella. It's not that big of a deal," Marta says, amusement playing her tone.

I stick out my tongue and shudder. "I heard you the first time."

Then I get to stand over an ancient-looking golden chalice until it stops bleeding...

And that's not even the worst of it. I shudder away the thought of what comes next.

It's like I've stepped out of suburbia and ended up on an episode of *Charmed* or something.

"So, tell us about this party you have planned," Stone offers with a sincere smile.

Marta glances at him with a confused expression.

He shrugs. "She wanted to be distracted."

Marta rolls her eyes.

"Lord help me," I mutter under my breath. Limbering up like I'm Rocky before a big fight, I hop up and down on my spot, rolling my head from side to side. "Okay, okay... Let's do this."

You got this, Ella. You got this. Nothin' to it.

Before I can talk myself out of it, I place the tip of the knife to the fleshy end of my left index finger. With a quick swipe, I slice it through my skin.

"Mother trucker," I curse, pressing my lips tight as the twinge of pain bolts through the end of my finger.

Blood surfaces immediately and I bend forward, letting it drop into the chalice of blessed wine or whatever. What I want to do is hop around, flapping like a lunatic until I stick my finger in my mouth.

"See, not so bad, was it?" Stone grins.

"Yeah, but I bet it'll be a bitch to type tomorrow," I mutter, watching the blood disappear into the red liquid already pooled inside the cup.

"It most certainly will not," Marta responds, tilting her head and suggesting I give her the knife back.

"Oh, right, super-healing to the rescue," I mutter, handing her the knife. When she takes it, I jam my finger into my mouth. Even now, the sting of the cut is beginning to fade.

Marta takes the knife, slicing through her finger like it was a cherry tomato going on tonight's salad. She doesn't even flinch. As her blood mixes with mine in the chalice of wine, she passes the knife on to Stone.

"So, have you and Clem got the whole thing planned out?" Stone continues with his previous conversation, even though I no longer need the distraction. With little fanfare, he also slices open his fingertip and drains the blood into the cup.

I shrug. "I suppose. We've only talked a couple of times but Clementine is pretty excited about it. Why haven't you guys ever done a party like this before? Is it really that weird?"

When the blood stops running, Stone licks his wound the same way I had. However, he holds it out and the thing has almost healed over completely already.

Lucky bastard.

He smirks at me like he caught wind of my thought.

Shit.

"I don't think many people wanted to party with Silas, for starters," Stone says, then his eyebrows knit together. "Or maybe it was just me."

"Definitely not just you," Marta says, picking up the chalice and swishing it around like she's about to do a wine taste test. "We have held gatherings in the past, but this one is certainly unusual."

"Why?" I snort. "It's just a barbecue."

"For starters, it's not necessarily pack-related," Stone says. "The mundane aspects of human life, like political holidays... They don't really touch us. You know? I mean, some of us have been around since before the United States was even a country. So..."

My eyes widen as I let that sink in. "Oh, right."

Until this very moment, I've never really pondered how long werewolves live.

"It is time to consummate the blood bond," Marta interjects, holding out the chalice to me.

Before I can get a grip, my face contorts in disgust. My stomach rolls at the idea of drinking a mixture tainted with all of our blood. It grosses me right the fuck out.

"You can't get sick from this. The diseases humans get through blood—they can't survive in our system," Stone says.

"How do you—" The words cut off when I remember what he does for a living.

He grins, placing a warm hand on the small of my back. "Trust me, as soon as it's done, you'll wonder why you didn't do it sooner."

I turn to face Marta and take the golden chalice from her. Holding it in both hands, it feels like I'm staring into the Holy Grail or something.

"Please tell me I chose wisely," I whisper to myself.

Stone chuckles softly, clearly getting my reference.

I shoot him a quick grin and lift the cup to my lips. Then, I take a sip and wait for whatever crazy energy will be unleashed the moment I do.

Surprisingly, it only tastes of strong wine, and not of blood. As I pull back the chalice, I stare at it with suspicion. Nothing inside me feels overtly different at all. In fact, I feel the same.

I turn to Marta, handing her the cup. "Was I supposed to feel something?"

Instead of responding, she lifts the chalice to her lips, closes her eyes, and takes her sip.

I turn to Stone and quirk an eyebrow.

He holds up a pointer finger, telling me to wait.

Inhaling a slow breath, I let my shoulders relax.

At least the worst is over.

Marta extends her hand, giving the cup over to Stone.

He takes it from her, then leans in close to whisper in my ear. "You might want to brace yourself."

I narrow my gaze.

But before I have the chance to open my mouth, he takes his sip. The moment he pulls the cup from his lips, a bright, intense light bursts from the center of my chest. It connects to Marta, then from Marta to Stone and back to me—like a triangle of vibrating blue energy. It's similar to the cord of light the night I chose them, but it pulsates between the three of us, growing brighter and brighter.

Then, when the connection between the three of us has gained enough momentum, a shockwave blasts out from the three of us like a spray of lightning bolts in every direction. Each bolt finds a pack member, linking them all back to the three of us.

The impact of it nearly knocks Seth off of his feet. Clementine, Albert, and the others press back into their chairs and hold onto their armrests for dear life.

As the energy connects with each of them, I feel every thought, impulse, and location streaming from them. The energy continues, finding the pack members wherever they are. One by one, I'm acutely aware of every single pack member like they're simply an extension of myself.

"This is so wiggy," I mutter, blinking back the intensity of it.

I thought the connection to the pack was strong before, but this...

Flitting my gaze between Marta and Stone, their expressions tell me it's nearly as profound for them, even if the feelings they're exuding wasn't doing it for them.

Marta nods, inhaling deeply. "I had heard from others in leadership of this... But the experience is vastly more impressive." She turns her hands over, inspecting them.

"Even knowing how it works, it's still a shock to the system," Stone says, shaking his head. "I feel like I have whiplash going from the Omega to Delta."

I chuckle. "Imagine how I feel. Human to Alpha is..."

"Crazy," Stone finishes.

"Oh, yeah." I nod.

Turning my hands over the way Marta had, I stare dumbfounded at my sliced fingertip. Not only is the wound healed, but there's no trace of it. No scar or anything...

"Wiggy," I repeat.

Seth walks over to us, planting a hand on Stone's shoulder. "It's good to be a cohesive pack again."

Albert raises his beer in salute. The two beside him do the same.

Clementine walks over to me with an enormous

grin on her face. "Welcome to the family." She wraps her arms around me, pulling me in tight.

I laugh, hugging her in return.

"The Portland Pack would have felt that," Marta says. "I would wager they'll think twice before trying to make another move."

"Let's hope so. The message would have been sent out far and wide," Stone agrees. "I'd be surprised if there was a pack in the state that didn't feel that."

"Now we just have one final thing to do to make it official," Clementine says, stepping back and nudging me with her shoulder. She grins triumphantly. "Tomorrow, I'm bringing you to get your Black Crater Pack tattoo."

CHAPTER 11

BRANDED
ELLA

"Can I get a tattoo, too?" Asher asks, his eyes aglow with the kind of anticipation only a naive teenager can bring to the equation.

"Absolutely not," I sputter, incredulous.

"Why not? I'll be eighteen next March," he says, mimicking my tone.

I plant my hands on my hips. "Then, if you still want one in March, be my guest."

He groans.

"How many more of these places are we going to go to?" Avery asks, blinking slowly.

This is obviously not her thing but I thought it would be one semi-normal part of pack life they could participate in. I want them to feel connected to this new me, while not having to deal so much with the world of weird that my life has become.

A tattoo is harmless—well, *mostly*.

Granted, neither of them realize we had to pick a supernatural tattoo shop that specializes in ink that'll stick around for me.

Yay, super-fast healing.

But we won't tell them about that.

"Yeah, what was wrong with the last two?" Clementine whines, dropping her arms like she's reverting to some sort of cavewoman version of herself.

I laugh and shake my head. "I don't know. They didn't have the right vibe. I need to click with whoever is gonna do this."

"When I said I'd bring you to get your tattoo, it was before I knew you'd be the pickiest Alpha on the entire planet. Seriously, it took less time to get Doug to commit and have babies," she mutters.

"Well, then pray this is the one," I say, shooting her a gigantic grin. I reach for the handle and open the door to *Serpent Tattoo*.

Clementine raises an eyebrow, evidently skeptical.

I hold the door open, brushing my hand out, and suggesting they all file in.

Asher is inside before I even take count, but Avery and Clementine look like they're ready to draw straws.

"Oh, for the love... *Go in!*" I declare, giving Avery *the look* and pointing.

She lopes inside, following after her brother.

Clementine gives the building a once-over and

winces slightly. "Are you sure you want to go in this one? It smells funny."

I point toward the inside as my response. While it has a burnt wood odor, to me, it just gives it the kind of ambiance that goes along with its name.

She sighs heavily and follows the kids.

Truth be told, this is the first one I wanted to check out. I like the Asian atmosphere and dragon motif. Something about it just screams, *get your beautiful tattoos here.*

However, Clementine had other recommendations, and rather than assuming I knew better than she did—I mean, she has lived here her whole life—I went along with her suggestions.

They just didn't fit.

If I'm going to brand my skin with a magical tattoo, I'm gonna make damn sure it feels right. If there's one thing I've learned in my forty-two years, it's to trust my instincts.

My spirits lift the second I walk in and the door closes behind me. The walls are painted in a deep, blood-red with black accent walls and a black texture painted over parts of the red. Everywhere you look there are various renditions of dragons. Some in paintings, some in statues... Even the lounge cushions on the couch in the waiting room depict the oriental dragon style.

Both Asher and Avery take a seat on the couch and Avery picks up one of the cushions, admiring it.

The air is thick with incense and the heady aroma makes me smile. It reminds me of when I was in my twenties and visited every New Age shop in San Diego, just because I could.

"Can I help you?" A woman with dark skin asks, entering the room from behind a curtain of red, black, and gold beads. She steps up to a counter that looks more like a hostess podium for a restaurant than a place to order a tattoo.

Walking over to her, it's clear she commands a presence. Her shoulders are broad and she has about as much added padding as I do, which instantly endears me to her.

Finally, a woman in the supernatural world who isn't built like a bodybuilder.

Plus, I can't help but marvel at the way her dark hair has been put in tiny braids that are pulled into a beautiful display on the top of her head. In between the strands of her natural black hair, literal golden strands are intermixed.

I suck in a breath and exhale it back out. "Yeah, I need a tattoo."

She laughs heartily. "Well, then I think you came to the right place, child. What are you looking to do?"

"I need something like this," I say, tugging out the piece of paper from my back pocket. Unfolding it, I slide the drawing of the Black Crater Pack design across the counter between us.

Her eyebrows shift up when she sees the image, then she raises her wide eyes to me.

It's obvious immediately that she knows what it symbolizes, which I take as a good sign.

Leaning in, I say, "I want this, but I'm thinking about adding a little to it. The moon is lovely, but I'd like to add a few dangling stars to the bottom. Kinda like this."

I grab a pencil from the desk and sketch it out.

"And of course, I'd need special ink," I say, leaning slightly over the counter and shooting her a knowing look.

She glances from me to Clementine and back again. "Are you sure you want *me* to do this?"

I surprise myself when the words pop out of my mouth before I've given much thought to them. "Yes, I would."

Again, she laughs. Shaking her head, she points at one of the chairs in the space behind her. "Well, I have a few minutes now, if you're ready."

I glance over my shoulder at Clementine who tries desperately to adjust the look of apprehension on her face.

"Are you okay?" I ask, shaking my head.

"Of course," she squeaks. "I'll—I'm gonna hang out with the kids." She points to where Asher and Avery now sit and walks quickly over to them.

What's gotten into you? I ask, broadcasting the thought to her.

She glances up and shakes her head. *I'm good.*

I narrow my gaze but decide to move on. She's got her panties in a bunch over something, but it's got nothing to do with me. So, whatever.

"My name's Sasha. I own this place," the woman in front of me says, taking a seat beside one of the larger tattoo lounge chairs.

I extend my hand. "Ella. I, uh—"

Do I tell her I'm the Alpha of the werewolf pack? Or is the tattoo enough of a giveaway?

I glance over at Clementine looking for some guidance, but she's buddied up to Avery and having a chat with her.

"You're the new Alpha in town, huh?" Sasha asks, breaking that ice.

I breathe out a sigh of relief. "Yes."

"I heard rumors a female was chosen, but I wasn't sure I believed them." She smiles softly, setting the drawing down on a tray beside her.

"Well, now you know."

She nods, tapping the drawing. "Okay, so Mrs. Alpha, where would you like this?"

"I'm not married," I say out of reflex.

Sasha's eyebrows lift again and a big toothy grin breaks across her face. "Even better. A female Alpha with no mate. What will the world come to next?"

I sit there for a moment, watching her, because I'm not sure what to say to that.

"So, where'll it be?" she repeats.

"Oh, right. Uhm, maybe right here?" I say, pointing to my left wrist.

"Have you ever been tatted before?" she asks with a crooked expression.

I shake my head. "No. First time."

"All right, then you might want this thing placed somewhere else. The wrist doesn't have much in the way of padding if you know what I mean." She grins at me and chuckles under her breath.

I narrow my eyes at her. "If a male Alpha came in here and said they wanted it on their wrist, would you be trying to talk him out of it?"

"First of all, I highly doubt a male Alpha would ever step foot in my shop. But for the sake of this conversation, if they did, they'd likely already have tatts, so I wouldn't have to say a thing." She blinks at me slowly.

"Thank you for your concern, Sasha, but I think I'll be fine," I say, squaring my shoulders and pulling my big girl panties, metaphorically speaking. I mean, after all, I just sliced my fingertip open and drank blood. I can do hard things.

She laughs. "Suit yourself."

For the next few moments, she sets to work, getting the tattoo gun and other items ready.

"Now, you know this has to be done in special ink, right?" I say, drumming the arm of my chair and trying to make conversation.

"Of course. I'm no amateur," Sasha says.

"Right, right," I say, shaking my head. "Sorry."

The fact that this is my first time and I'm not sure what to expect must be getting to me. It's almost as bad as last night's blood bond ritual. I just want it over with.

"Just relax and focus on something else while I set to work. Okay?" Sasha says, scooting her stool up so she can get closer to my wrist. "And whatever you do, try not to move."

My heartbeat thumps unevenly in my chest and the room is suddenly much too warm. "Okay."

I flit my gaze to the crew on the couch, wishing they'd come over to keep me company. I'm just about to ask them, but think better of it. They're all doing well and not freaking out on each other. Best to let sleeping dogs lie and all that.

"Are they yours? The young ones, that is?" Sasha asks, following my gaze.

I nod. "Yeah. They're here for moral support."

Sasha nods. "That's nice—you know, to have that. Okay, hold still now."

She starts up the tattoo gun and I close my eyes, waiting for the first hint of pain. Interestingly, I feel a slight tug, but the burning sensation I expected never comes. I glance down, just to be sure she's started working—and she has.

"So weird," I mutter, staring at her hand as she outlines the crescent moon and moves on to the tribal design of the inside.

She pulls the gun away and glances up. "What's weird?"

"I can't feel anything. Like, nothing—"

Her expression says she's as surprised as I am.

"Well, that's good news then." She smirks at me and drops her gaze back to her work.

When she has the whole piece outlined, she dabs at it with a cloth and looks up. "Still good so far?"

I nod. "Right as rain."

She chuckles. "People still say that?"

My cheeks feel like they burst into flames but I say, "Obviously."

"So, do you like being Alpha?" Sasha asks, continuing to color in the rest of the tattoo.

I think on that a moment and the hesitation is enough to make her pause.

"I mean, yes. But it's still weird, you know?" I confess.

"I would imagine. You were human before, yes? Bitten?" she asks.

My eyebrows rise into my hairline. "Wow, news does travel fast. Yes, I was bitten."

"You've certainly stirred things up, then. Eh?" She continues to work, her hand extremely steady as she embeds the magical ink into my skin.

"I guess I have."

"Well, good. Things were in need of a swift kick in the—" she clamps her mouth shut, then looks over her shoulder at the kids and Clementine. "Sorry, I don't mean to offend your friend. She was the last Alpha's mate, wasn't she?"

"She was." I nod. "And don't worry, she's in agreement with that statement, too. Granted, it would have been nice if change came without meaning the death of her hus—*mate*."

I'm still not used to saying the terms used by the pack just yet.

Sasha tips her head in acknowledgment. "That must be very difficult."

"It has been. She's strong, though," I say, chancing another glance.

If Clementine is eavesdropping on our conversation, she's doing a great job not showing any signs.

"You all are. I admire the wolves of this community. You're all very—*loyal*."

I catch Sasha's intense stare and hold it for a beat. It's like she wants to say more, but doesn't know how to say it.

"Well, not all of us. I mean, Silas wasn't too great at loyalty," I mutter, dropping my gaze back to the tattoo.

She nods, falling silent. For the next few minutes, she works on the tattoo, not even pausing to look up at the drawing. It's like she's burned it into her memory.

Before I know it, she pulls back the tattoo gun, tilting her head from side to side.

"Done," she proclaims.

"Already?" I pull my wrist closer to my face, getting a good look at it.

It's absolutely *perfect*.

If I could have plucked the idea from my head and implanted it in hers, we couldn't have gotten a better outcome.

"This is wonderful," I say, practically gushing. "How did you do that?"

She laughs. "Wouldn't be a very good tattoo artist if I couldn't tattoo art."

"No, I mean, it's *perfect*. Thank you."

"You're very welcome." Sasha pats my knee, then takes off her latex gloves.

I slide off the chair and stretch. "How much do I owe you?"

"Oh, no. On the house. I couldn't possibly charge the new Alpha in town," Sasha says, holding up her hands.

"No, I insist—"

She shakes her head and crosses her arms over her chest. "Nope."

I narrow my gaze, knowing a brick wall when I see one. "Fine. But you'll need to at least let me take you out for coffee or drinks or something."

Her eyes widen. "You'd wanna have coffee with me?"

"Of course," I snicker. "Why wouldn't I?"

"It just—I," she starts, shaking her head. "I mean, I'd love to have coffee with you sometime, Ella."

"Great," I beam back at her. "Thank you again. Truly, this is incredible."

"Pleasure was all mine," she says.

For the briefest of moments, I swear, her eyes sparkle with flecks of real gold. But before I can tell for sure, they're gone.

I shoot her a side-eye but meander over to the lounge area.

"Guys, look at what Sasha did. Isn't she a tattoo genius?" I say, extending my wrist out for the three of them to see.

"Nice, Mom," Asher nods in approval. "Can I get one?"

"Eighteen," I mutter.

"Lemme see," Avery says, contorting over Clementine to get a look. "Pretty."

"Looks awesome. Now, can we get outta here?" Clementine asks, pushing to a stand and practically dragging me to the door.

I follow after her, surprised by her sudden desire to leave. She's the reason we're here in the first place.

However, as I tune in to her, deep apprehension rolls off of her in waves. She's not happy about being here and she wants to get far, far away.

What in the world's gotten into her?

CHAPTER 12

DO WHAT YOU LOVE

ELLA

"**W**hy is this so hard?" I groan, letting my forehead slump to the desk.

The deadline for my article has come and gone and I'm still staring at a mostly blank page. No matter what I do, I just can seem to get the words to flow. It's like there's a physical block between my brain and the work I need to do.

Maybe I have *mental dysfunction*.

As if my own admonishments weren't enough, I've already gotten two gentle reminders and one nasty-gram from my boss. He's expecting the article today. No more delays.

If I can't get this thing to cooperate, I can only imagine what he's gonna do.

I've always been a team player and never missed a deadline before. So, I'm hoping this blemish on my record will be short-lived.

Of course, it all hinges on me pulling my head from my butt long enough to write this damn thing. It's just that *it's sooooo boring*.

I stare at my hands, clasped together in my lap. Why can't they just do the work without needing my brain to be in charge? That sure would be handy.

Like the dork I am, I chuckle at the pun.

Sitting up with far too much effort, I turn over my left wrist, admiring the artistry of the Black Crater Pack tattoo.

I've never been a tattoo person, but I have to admit, it's a thing of beauty. It came out exactly the way I wanted.

I still don't know what Clementine's problem was. Sasha was a sweetheart. A little quirky, I guess, but no worse than the two of us. And she was a certainly pro with that tattoo gun.

So bizarre.

What's even weirder is that Clem wouldn't even talk about it. Instead, she kept blowing me off and focusing on the kids. If I were more adept at sifting through the thoughts and feelings coming at me, I may have been able to suss out the problem, but this new connection to the pack is still far too overwhelming. Instead, I've tried tuning it out more than letting it all in.

Plus, I don't overly want to pry. If roles were reversed, I wouldn't want the pack's Alpha rooting around in my mind just because she could. That would be rude.

For all I know, Clementine's weird vibe has something to do with Doug.

My gaze drifts back to the laptop and the taunting cursor.

"I need coffee," I declare, pushing myself away from the desk.

Of course, the evil cursor blinks ominously at me. Crumpling my face, I close the laptop and shove it into my laptop bag.

Coffee shop it is.

And who knows? Maybe the change of scenery will kick something loose? Wouldn't be the first time.

The drive to the coffee shop is nothing short of a blur. I barely even register that I've left my house before I'm putting the Highlander in park.

My mind is tumbling through thoughts ranging from "How the hell am I gonna finish this article?" to "I wonder if the Portland Pack has left yet?" And pretty much everything in between.

Add on top the mixture of all the thoughts and emotions from the pack members, and it's like I'm constantly finding myself in a crowded room with everyone talking at the same time.

No wonder I can't focus.

Plus, I'm still low key wondering what's going on between me and Stone.

There's just...*too much.*

I lean over and grab my laptop bag and purse from the passenger seat. Then, I make my way into the coffee shop like the woman on a mission I am.

At least this time, I'm wearing a bra. So, I consider it a definite win.

However, this time, the mission is to get coffee and not leave until the article has written itself.

When I get inside, the place is surprisingly quiet. There are only a handful of people and they're all enjoying their caffeine fix in relative silence. There's only one table with two people and they're both staring at their phones rather than speaking to one another.

I guess the 2 p.m. crowd isn't as rambunctious as the morning java crew.

Shaking my head, I walk up to the counter. The barista must be new because he isn't someone I've seen here before. He's got a chill vibe that contradicts his spikey blond hair.

He glances up as I approach, but doesn't say anything.

"Hey, can I get a medium light roast coffee and a chocolate cake pop?" I ask, shooting him a big smile.

He quirks a sardonic eyebrow and declares, "We're out of light roast."

"Oh, shit. That sucks. Um, let me see..." I say, raising my gaze to the menu plastered in bright neon marker behind him. "How about a medium, uh—"

He crosses his arms over his torso.

I lower my eyebrows and keep searching the sea of beverage options. Truth be told, they all sound like they should be part of a nature hike and not a drink meant to keep me awake for the next few hours.

Finally, I shrug and plant my purse on the counter between us. "Can I just get a Campfire Mocha with a double shot of espresso?"

The guy looks mildly impressed as he starts typing in the order. "Medium for that, too?"

"Yup," I say, eyeing the space and finding a quiet table in the corner that has an outlet for my laptop.

"What kind of milk?"

"Almond?" I respond, glancing back in his direction.

"Is that what you want or was it a question?" The barista asks, shifting his gaze from the screen to me.

"If you've got it, I want it," I say, giving him two thumbs up.

He gives me a once over, then nods to himself, and gives me my total.

After what feels like the longest episode of "Will she ever get to sit down?" I finally have my coffee and treat in hand and make my way to the table in the corner.

I set my laptop bag on the table and take a seat facing the wall of windows. For the first few minutes, I sit alone, eating my cake pop and drinking my coffee.

Rather than looking at the laptop or stressing about it, I tune into the constant hum of feelings coming from the pack. While there's still a low level of alertness, the main vibe is calm and that makes me feel good. Since I took over, everyone has been pretty cool with it. With of course, the little blip as they waited for me to pick my crew.

My mind drifts to the upcoming party and the only thing I wish was different was my personal level of connection with each of the pack members. I get a sense there are some I've never even met yet. Which is totally weird.

But I suppose it's no different from being a CEO and having employees who get hired in your multinational company or something.

I shake my head. Look at me. Comparing myself to a big CEO.

Taking another sip of coffee, my gaze drifts around the room. Only the couple staring on their phones and one other patron remains.

I glance at my laptop bag and sigh. "It's now or never, Ella."

Somehow I doubt it's going to be much quieter than it is now. If I can get my head down and focus, I could hammer this thing out in a couple of hours.

She needs to know...

The thought pulls me up short midway through grabbing my laptop.

Because I wasn't tuned into it, the owner of the thought slips past me too quickly. I scrunch my face and shrug.

If there's something important I need to be worried about, I have no doubt the news will find me. In the meantime, music is in order.

I reach into my purse, pulling out my ages-old earbuds set. Of course, the damn thing is so tangled I consider throwing them in the trash. However, since facing the article is a worst prospect, I take the time to untangle them. Thankfully, I only question my life choices twice.

After connecting them to my phone, I promise myself that if I can write this damn article, I'll treat myself to a new pair of Bluetooth earbuds.

How can she not sense it?

I crank the music, letting it drown out the background noise of the pack the way I used to drown out my kids fighting in the next room.

After listening to two of my favorite motivational songs, I pull out my notebook and review the notes I've already taken for the article.

It all seems relatively basic but it's the starting point that's just not working for me.

Any other time, I'd dive straight into the causes of erectile dysfunction and why the new drug would benefit the population. But it just feels like that setup falls flat—no pun intended.

I want more. Like whatever I write needs to be more interesting somehow, but I just can't seem to find the vantage point and have no clue where to start.

Instead, I try out half a dozen opening sentences, each one worse than the one before it.

"Fuck," I mutter, pushing my laptop away and dropping my head back.

My headphones pop out and drop to my lap like they were bungee cords. Exhaling loudly, I stare at the false ceiling, noticing the water spots that have formed on some of the tiles and trying to decide if they look like anything interesting.

"You look like you're having a helluva time with whatever you're working on."

Startled, I look around to find Jinx, the woman from my walk the other day, grinning over at me. She's taken up residence with her own laptop and coffee cup at the table beside me. How long she's been sitting there is beyond me. I'd been so engrossed in starting this thing that I'd had tunnel vision.

"Yeah, I think I broke my brain," I lament, frowning at my laptop.

She chuckles and takes a sip of her coffee. "Whatcha working on?"

I cross my eyes slightly and sigh. "An article about a potential new erectile dysfunction drug."

Her eyebrows raise into her bright orange hairline. "Wow. I wouldn't have guessed that one."

"Not surprised," I chuckle."It's boring as hell."

"It does seem like dry material," she makes a face, "I mean, it's great news for those who need it, but man..."

"Right?" I say. "It's not a bad thing, it's just... I don't know. These types of articles aren't fun anymore."

"They were fun?" Jinx asks with a hint of surprise.

"Well, not *fun*, per se. But I liked the research and understanding how different medications interact with people," I mutter, leaning back in my chair. "They're not all about E.D."

"What changed?"

"I did, I guess." I shrug.

Behind Jinx, the blond barista walks over to the table where the two people were sitting. They must have finally gotten off their phones long enough to vacate the building because they're gone. He sets to work, placing the dirty cups, plates, and a random napkin on a tray to take away. As he grabs it and spins around, his feet don't manage to make the transition. Instead, the tray flips out of his hand, and while he catches himself on the table, it's safe to say, the dishes are toast as they shatter across the floor.

"Shit," he spits, watching in horror at the new mess to clean up.

My eyebrows rise.

"Well, in my experience, it's always best to let go of things that no longer bring you joy," Jinx says sagely, ignoring the commotion behind her completely.

I shift my gaze to her. "Huh?"

A slow grin creeps across her face. "If it's not jerkin' your chain anymore—God, such a good pun for this—you should find something new. You know, come to think of it..."

Stone walks into the coffee shop and my attention snaps to him. There's a magnetic quality to him that draws me from whatever I'm currently doing to wherever he is. It's both exciting and incredibly unfortunate for whomever I happen to be talking to.

I sigh contently as he approaches, enjoying the way his muscles move under his tight-fitting black t-shirt and jeans.

As he gets closer, his face darkens and my content bubble bursts.

"Ella, can I have a word?" He shifts his gaze from me to Jinx and back again. Then he adds, "*Privately*."

CHAPTER 13

ROCK HER WORLD
STONE

When Stone heard that Ella had been making friends outside of the pack, he hadn't thought anything of it. After all, it wasn't as if they were forced to only fraternize with pack members.

However, as more accounts came in, his concern grew. It seemed that Ella wasn't only a magnet for werewolves and their drama—she was a magnet for all manner of supernatural creatures. Some of which, she needed to be insanely careful around.

There was only one problem.

She knew nothing about any of them.

Up until now, Stone hadn't even considered having one of the "larger-world" conversations with her. She had enough to deal with, so he was more focused on letting Ella and her kids get settled into their new norm. It was bad enough that she was thrust into this wolf pack dynamic.

But when Clementine came to him, he knew the reports weren't being exaggerated. His sister rarely took issue with relationships, but Ella's choice for her tattoo artist had shaken his sister. Especially when the vibe coming off the tattoo artist should have been enough to bounce Ella right out of her establishment. It had certainly done that for Clem, by the sounds of it.

Instead, it appeared Ella was making friends in all the wrong places, and it was going to put her leadership—*if not her life*—in jeopardy.

The moment he walked into the coffee shop and saw who she was chatting with, it took an enormous amount of reserve not to hurl the creature out the door.

If nothing else, it should have known better than to buddy up with the Black Crater Alpha. The audacity of the thing.

While Ella might be oblivious, the creature certainly was not.

He kept his focus solely on her as they left the coffee shop and headed outside.

"What is it, Stone? Is everyone okay?" Ella asked, concern flashing in her beautiful brown eyes.

He blinked rapidly, trying to figure out how to word things in a way that would make the most sense. Unfortunately, anything of value fled his brain the moment they were alone together.

Ella narrowed her eyes and he felt her presence creeping over his awareness as she felt for answers before he could speak them. For a moment, he pondered whether she was doing it purposely or if it came naturally, like so many other aspects.

Stone heaved a sigh and pointed to the outdoor patio table. "I think you should sit."

Alarm crossed her features. "What's going on?"

"Seriously, I think we should sit—" he said, again jabbing his index finger toward the table.

She huffed a breath, clearly annoyed, but walked to the table. As soon as she was seated, she crossed her arms over her torso and gave him a stare that forced an involuntary shudder from him.

"There are some things..." he began, as he took his seat opposite her. His eyebrows knit together but knew he needed to just rip the bandaid off. "Ella, we need to talk about who you've been interacting with lately. It's gotten some of the pack—"

"Oh, my god. Not you, too. Seriously?" Ella said indignantly. She dropped her hands to the table and leaned forward. "What is with you guys?"

"You don't understand." He tapped his right eyebrow and wondered how he was going to get through to her. He knew how independent she was and the last thing he wanted to do was come across like he was trying to control her.

"I understand just fine. The pack is a snobby bunch and they expect me to fall in line with that snobbery.

Well, I hate to break it to you, but I'm not Silas. And furthermore—"

"Ella, that woman in there, the one you were just talking with," Stone interjected, pointing toward the windows, "is a *chaos demon.*"

Ella's rant stopped and her features went slack. "S-say that again?"

He leaned forward and reached out for her hands. She offered them up, but he could tell it was more out of confusion than the actual desire to do so.

"I know we should have had this talk sooner. It's just that..."

This conversation felt eerily similar to the day when he had to show her he was a werewolf because she was about to become one, too. Rocking her world seemed to be a pattern for Stone—only not in a good way.

Ella's eyebrows rose and her eyes went distant. Then, she sighed heavily. "You know, that actually explains a lot."

"It does?"

"Only in a *'welcome to my new life'* kinda way. But yes." She nodded, locking eyes with him. "Everywhere that woman goes, chaos ensues. A guy tripped—hell, *I tripped*. Another one spilled coffee down himself. A kid lost a wheel on his scooter. The barista in there nearly took out a table and ended up flinging everything he was trying to pick up. Seriously, I've never seen anything like it." She huffed out a laugh and shook her head.

"So you understand why it's so important to be careful who you—"

She swiped a hand in the air. "Eh, she's harmless."

Stone lowered his eyebrows. "She's a *demon.*"

"So what? I spent over a decade with my ex. Trust me, I'm good at spotting evil when I see it now," Ella said, glancing into the coffee shop. "She's not it."

Stone blew out a puff of air. How was he going to get her to understand what was at stake here?

Suddenly, she burst out in laughter, slapping at her thigh. "I get it now..."

"Get what?" Stone asked, not quite following her.

"Jinx. Her nickname is *Jinx.*" She continued to laugh until tears formed in her eyes. "It was staring me in the face the whole time. I wonder if she knew I didn't know..." Again she glanced into the coffee shop.

The demon was still sitting with her back faced out to them as she worked on her laptop.

"There are *others*," Stone said, tiptoeing into the larger conversation.

Ella glanced back in his direction.

"If you've heard of it, chances are..." He cleared his throat. "They exist."

Her eyebrows flew into her hairline and she held up a hand between them. "Wait, wait... You mean *everything* is real?"

Stone winced slightly and ran his thumb over the stubble below his lip. "Yeah, pretty much."

"Vampires?" She shot back as she narrowed her eyes.

He nodded.

"Fairies?"

He shrugged. "Probably. Can't say I've run into any, though."

"Nessy?"

She was making fun now. He could feel it in her energy.

His expression deadpanned and he leaned back. "You know, I'm glad you're taking this all in stride. I was concerned you were going to be more upset."

"Don't get me wrong, there is definitely a part of me that's running around with the head explosion emoji," she chuckled. "But if I'm honest, I'm not so naive to think that if one supernatural group is real that the others aren't at least possible. You know?"

"Makes sense," Stone agreed.

Ella tapped the edge of the table with her middle finger. "While contemplating it and *knowing it* are two different things, I kinda feel like I can't just bury my head in the sand. I have a bigger responsibility now."

"Speaking of responsibility—" He began, hoping to segue back into why she needs to be more careful.

"Stone, I appreciate what you're trying to do. Really," she said, cutting him off. "But I'm a big girl and can make my own mind up about people—or beings.

Whatever. I don't need you, or anyone else to tell me when someone is bad news. I also don't need anyone's approval of my friends. If the pack doesn't like it, then they can just suck it. My every move was controlled once before and I promised myself I'd never become that person ever again."

"I get that. It's just—" he pressed his lips tight as he fought the warring emotions inside himself, "some beings aren't friendly. Meaning, there are unspoken rules. Chaos demons, for example..."

"I don't care," she said with a shrug. "If they're nice to me, I'll be nice back. It's always been my rule and I'm not about to change it now."

A growl rode his next words. "Ella, as Alpha—"

"As Alpha, *I decide*, Stone," she said, enveloping her words as a command.

His mouth snapped shut and he tipped his head in acknowledgment of it.

There was no point in fighting her on this. She had made up her mind and it would only force her to dig in further if he fought it. The last thing he wanted was to push her toward them—or away from him.

"Ella, all I ask is that you be careful," he whispered.

She reached out and placed her hand over the top of his. "I appreciate that."

There was something in the way that she carried herself, in the way that she smiled at him, and it made Stone's worries dissipate. So far, Ella had known what she was doing and no one had been hurt.

He glanced down and noticed a hint of her Black Crater Pack tattoo on her wrist.

"May I see your tattoo?" he asked. After everything that had been going on lately, Stone had had barely enough time to connect with her, let alone keep up with everything.

Ella smiled and rotated her wrist over so he could see it. While the tattoo was still a little pink, it had almost healed over completely. He had to admit to himself, even if he wouldn't have chosen the same tattoo artist, she had done an incredible job.

The signature moon of the Black Crater Pack was remarkable and the decorative embellishments Ella had added were just the right touch. It spoke of who she was and the way she would lead. Strong and centered, but with a soft, feminine approach, as well.

He grinned and rubbed his thumb along the edge of her wrist, careful not to touch the tattoo itself for now. "Looks great."

Ella beamed. "I know, right? I have to admit, I wasn't much of a tattoo person, but I think I could be converted."

A smile crept upon Stone's face. He could imagine Ella with more tattoos. Though, she certainly wouldn't need them to maintain her mystique. At least, not for him.

She sighed into his touch. "I wish I could just sit here and relax into your touch for hours, but I better get back inside. I have an article past deadline and if I don't finish it, my boss is gonna kill me."

Stone shook his head, pulling back to himself. "No, I understand. But we'll have to make some plans to get together soon."

A little color swept through her cheeks and he sensed the shift in her as her mind strayed to their last few moments alone. He didn't hear her thoughts but he could feel the way they made her squirm.

"Yes, I'd like that very much." She grinned, sighed to herself, and stood up. "But first, *duty calls.*"

CHAPTER 14
STRAIGHT TO THE POINT
ELLA

I wonder how many different kinds of supernatural beings there are? And how do I know one when I see them?

Glancing over at Jinx, I'm surprised at how much it makes sense to find out what she is. I haven't bothered talking to her about it yet but the knowledge of what she is comforts me. Which is totally weird, all things considered.

I mean, she's a *demon*.

Yet, for some bizarre reason, that doesn't automatically equate to evil in my mind and I don't know why.

However, if there's one thing I've learned in my years on this planet, it's to trust my instincts.

My only concern is why I'm just learning about this now. It seems like the others can sense other supernatural beings, but I'm not picking up anything unusual.

Is it a newbie thing?

I eye the clock and close my laptop with a groan. Rather than staying focused on the task at hand, I've barely hit five hundred words on the article. Now it's time to pick up Avery from the mall.

Technically, I should have been there a few minutes ago. So, that's super.

In all of my years writing for *Pharma Formulary*, this is the first time I've really been at a loss. I don't know if it's because I'm so distracted, keep getting interrupted, or if it is just old news now and I want to reach for more.

Probably all of the above.

Goodness knows, the realizations slapping me upside the head as of late are far more interesting. They're also far more engaging. My brain just can't seem to get enough of it and despite trying to coax myself into focusing, I keep finding myself pondering this new world around me.

Something in my gut tells me I'm going to need to look for a new job soon. Even if I can manage this article, there will be more, and I can't live with each one being as painful as the last.

However, I know enough about this company to know there's definitely more where this came from and they *will be* as painful as the last.

I wish being Alpha was a paid gig.

"You leaving already?" Jinx asks, glancing up at

me. Her inquisitive green eyes survey me as I pack everything up.

I nod. "Yeah, I gotta get my kid. She's been at the mall most of the day and I promised I'd get her at four."

"Did you finish your article?" Jinx asks, sliding into a smirk.

I stick out my tongue. "No, but I'll finish it at home. *I hope.*"

"You know—" she begins.

Suddenly, my phone springs to life, buzzing in my pocket. "Hang on," I say, holding up a finger and pulling it out to answer it. "Hello?"

"Mom, where are you?" Avery asks from the other end. There's an edge of panic in her voice but nothing too severe. She's probably just surprised I wasn't there early like I usually am.

"I'm almost there, sweetie," I say, pulling my laptop bag's strap over my shoulder. "Everything okay?"

"Yeah, I just thought you'd be here already. It's after four."

"I know. Sorry, sweetie. I was just trying to wrap up this article," I say with a slight wince.

Jinx chuckles as I make a face and point to the door. She nods and shoos me with her hands.

I wave at her and head out, weaving my way in and out of the tables.

"See you in a few minutes," I say, reaching for the door.

"Kay, bye." She hangs up without much fanfare.

When I get outside, I race for the Highlander. Luckily, the mall is only a couple of minutes from the coffee shop. By the time I get there, my mind has already found a way to meander back to the conversation with Stone.

The sheer number of times I tried to tune into Jinx and sense her innate magic was pretty crazy. But no matter how I focused, she just felt...*normal*.

I don't understand it.

Why can't I sense other supernatural beings?

It's gotta be because I'm new.

Is there some sort of supernatural being class I could take to learn more about this world I've stepped into?

Shaking my head, I put the vehicle into park and reach over to the passenger seat to grab my laptop bag. I cram it into the space behind my seat, then open my door. Then, I make my way to the mall entrance to hunt for my daughter.

Thankfully, Avery is sitting on a bench just inside the door.

"Hey, Avery. Ready to go?" I say, walking up to her.

She stands up with a couple of small bags and nods. "Yeah."

"Get anything good?" I ask, pointing to the bags.

"Eh, not really. I was hoping to get a new outfit,

but didn't find anything I liked," she says. "But I did get a new pair of shoes and a couple of books."

I snicker softly. "And those aren't good?"

"Well, they're fine. Just not what I was hoping to leave here with."

"Got it."

I guide the two of us out of the mall and toward our vehicle. Or, at least, where I thought our vehicle should be.

Pulling up short, I spin on my spot.

"You're lost? Seriously? Mom, you just parked the car," Avery snickers. "It's been like three minutes."

"Be quiet, Minion. I'm focusing," I say, pressing a fingertip to her lips.

She shakes her head and crosses her arms over her chest. Her bags jangle from her left wrist.

"Ah, yes. It's this way," I say, switching directions and dragging her along.

Thankfully, this time, I got the right row. Our Highlander comes into view and I breathe a sigh of relief.

"See, I still got it," I say, shooting her a cheesy grin.

She rolls her eyes and I swear, I have a flashback of her when she was four.

Laughing to myself, I unlock the vehicle and open the back so she can drop her bags.

"There's only two of them, Mom. I'll just sit with them," she says, shaking her head and walking around to her seat.

"You're welcome," I mutter, closing it back up again.

I walk around to my side, but as I reach out for my handle, a strange feeling rushes over me.

Turning around, I come face to face with Philip—Alpha of the Portland Pack.

A slow grin creeps across his dark features.

I inhale sharply and close my car door. "Can I help you, Philip?"

Despite the way things ended last time, there's still an edge of anxiety that rolls through me when he steps forward and into my personal space.

"Ella, it's lovely to see you again," he says.

I eye the space behind him, surprised to find him alone.

"Where is the rest of your pack?" I ask.

He shrugs. "They're nearby."

I quirk an eyebrow. "Mhmm. So, what can I do for you?"

"Straight to the point. I like it," he says, his deep booming laugh echoing through the parking lot.

I exhale and cross my arms.

Despite his size and demeanor, I refuse to be threatened by him. Stone would probably tell me I'm a fool and Marta—well, she'd expect me to call the entire pack here.

Philip drops his hands to his side and paces a bit in front of me. I look over my shoulder to check on Avery. Instead of sitting on her phone as she would normally be doing right now, her wide brown eyes are tracking Philip.

"You're scaring my daughter again," I declare, a low rumble reverberating through me.

"If I were here with ill intentions, I wouldn't be alone," he says, shooting me a knowing look.

"Then what is it?"

His dark eyebrows crowd together as he considers his words carefully. "Ella, you are a strong woman—any pack would be proud to have you as their leader."

I narrow my gaze, wondering where all this buttering up is leading.

"Since our last encounter," he continues, "I haven't been able to stop thinking about you."

For the first time since this conversation started, panic jolts through me.

If this guy is going to get all sentimental on me...

"You and I—we would make a formidable partnership," he says, his brown eyes sparkling with excitement.

I tilt my head to the side. "Philip, I'm flattered, but—"

"You should hear me out," he says, breaking through my announcement.

I sigh heavily, doubting very much that I want to hear what he has to say.

"As you know, I am somewhat known for my collection of powerful women," he says, his lips sliding into a sideways grin.

I nod. "I'm aware."

"I'm not suggesting you become just one of them. Before I met you, yes, I admit that was the plan. But now, I'd like for you to be *more*." A rumble rolls through him and he prowls forward.

Instinctively, I hold out a hand stopping him from getting any closer. "Whoa, there. Philip, I'm flattered, truly. But that's not gonna happen."

He pulls up short, confusion flicking through his features. "You are in need of a mate. I am willing to take you as mine. What more is there to discuss? Think of the territory gains for the both of us."

I have to physically stop myself from snickering. "Philip, as lovely an opportunity as this might be, it's not how I plan to lead my pack. Not everything is about getting more."

"I only have one other mate and she will be happy to welcome you in if that's what you're worried about," he says, genuinely trying to sort out my reasoning.

"As lovely as that sounds," I begin, internally shuddering the thought away, "I don't want to be one of many. And to be honest, for me, there's another—"

As soon as I think of Stone, it's like a ball of energy strikes me in my torso. Suddenly, I feel him on the move.

Shit.

He narrows his eyes and spits, "The white wolf?"

My eyes widen.

Was it that obvious?

"Maybe? I don't know just yet," I admit. "There's definitely something there. But truth be told, I'm not into rushing it."

There's an anxious air to Stone as he races in this direction—clearly in wolf form. I didn't intend to call him to me and if he arrives to see Philip, goodness only knows how things could get worse.

The last thing I need is a testosterone fight.

Philip frowns. "But he's a no one. Until you came into power, he was an Omega. He has nothing to offer you."

"First of all, who are you to say what he has to offer? Secondly, how dare you assume what it is I want. I may be new to this gig, but I assure you, I am firm in my desire to do things my way," I say, staring him directly in his eyes.

For a moment, those dark eyes flash a warning but it dissipates when I don't look away.

He steps forward, placing a hand on my elbow. "Ella, you must see reason."

Slowly, I drop my gaze to his hand and back up. "Kindly remove your hand."

He does as I ask and relief floods through me. Philip might be persistent but he's not like Silas.

"My answer is no, Philip," I say, imbuing each word with the power rising in my center.

He takes a slight step back, still confused by my refusal.

"It's time for you to go home," I announce. "And funnily enough, the same goes for me."

Unfortunately, it's too late.

Stone's wolf bursts into the parking lot, racing for the two of us at an unearthly speed.

CHAPTER 15
THE CALLING
STONE

When Stone felt Ella's call, he hadn't even stopped to question it.

She wanted him and it was important. That was all he needed to know.

He had hit the woods and shifted within seconds.

As he ran, his thoughts entangled with hers, growing until they were a palpable force. It throbbed in the center of his chest and summoned him—*and only him*—like a beacon to her.

She hadn't called the pack as a whole, and at first, he didn't know what that meant.

He tried not to let the moments when he caught her confused and concerned thoughts distract him. In his mind, getting to her as quickly as possible was paramount. It was much harder to ignore when his vision flashed back and forth between what she was seeing and what he was experiencing where he was.

But that was impossible. *Wasn't it?*

Yet, although she hadn't spoken directly to him through the pack link, somehow he knew Philip had cornered Ella with intentions of claiming her. Stone could see the man standing before her, telling her how he wanted to take her as a mate and expand his territory.

Fury coiled in the center of Stone's being.

Mine.

He had never been the possessive type but something had changed. Even if he couldn't understand it fully, he embraced the feeling and let it guide him. He'd be damned if he let Philip take her. Especially since it would be against her will.

She called *Stone.*

His wolf swelled with pride about that fact, but he cursed himself for taking things so slow with her. He had only wanted to give Ella time to get used to her new life but he knew better than most how outside packs would view it. Hell, how *wolves in general* would view it.

If they were fated, as Clementine believed—and as he was now beginning to believe—severing a bond like that before it had been claimed could be catastrophic for them both. And especially for the one rejected.

Not imprinting with a fated mate would be seen as weakness in the shifter world. Nothing should be able to keep them apart until the bond had been sealed. It was animal instinct in its purest sense.

Hesitation was an opening and any Alpha with sense would view it as a challenge of a lifetime. They would be more than happy to move swiftly and remedy his weakness with their strength. And if her wolf agreed, she would allow it and then be lost to him.

When Philip hadn't taken his pack back to Portland, it should have been a warning to Stone.

What had he been thinking?

He, of all people, should have known better. Silas's betrayal should have been lesson enough.

Yet, he had fought the urge to claim her all the same, and he had felt her fight the urge as well. It hadn't mattered to him that she didn't technically know what was happening. She needed time and he was happy to give it to her.

However, that didn't mean he hadn't been consumed by the urge more each day, building, thread by thread, like a thick rope that connected him to her. It had grown exponentially since their close encounter and with every moment that passed, he wanted nothing more than to get her alone and take her as his own.

He felt it grow for her as well but they hadn't had time to discuss things. So many things had gotten in the way.

Why could nothing go the way it was planned?

Stone. The call pulsed again and washed over him.

In her time of need, when a powerful Alpha was trying to lay claim to her, Ella wanted him. She may not understand the rules, but somewhere inside her, she had already made a decision.

She wanted him.

His heart beamed, even amidst the white-hot fury.

He knew damn well if she was his fated mate, it would explain her calling—and this connection.

For the two of them, it would be as natural as breathing. They were two halves of the same whole.

Stone pushed himself to run faster.

The mall was farther from his house than he would have liked, but he didn't let that stop him. Instead, he ran faster than he had in his whole life.

When Stone arrived on the scene, Ella was still in her human form—as was Philip.

He took it as a good sign that the Portland Alpha was not ready to make a scene in such a public place.

"It's time for you to go home. And funnily enough, the same goes for me," Ella said.

Stone felt her recognition of his arrival and a warm wave of relief flowed between the two of them. She turned to him and held out a hand. While she didn't say anything out loud or through their connection, her command still came through loud and clear.

Stone slowed and walked up to them both until he stood by her side. Despite trying to stay calm, his hackles rose. It took everything he had not to bare his teeth and go for Philip's jugular.

As Delta, he knew he had nowhere near the power to take on Philip, but his connection to Ella damned near overrode his logical brain.

Philip's eyebrow arched and he turned back to Ella. "It would appear he's very protective of you."

"I know I'm new at this, but from my experience, that's a wolf thing," Ella declared.

Her voice was even and centered and it calmed Stone's agitation a bit.

Philip tilted his head to the side. "True." He planted his discerning gaze on Stone. "But it's more than that."

Ella huffed a laugh. "And you know that how? By looking at him? Are you psychic, too?"

A slow smirk emerged on Philip's face. "Perhaps."

"Mkay," Ella muttered, crossing her arms over her chest.

"If I am wrong, then where are the rest of your numbers? Surely an Alpha who felt threatened would have called more to her?" Philip asked, narrowing his gaze on her.

Stone's tail twitched. Philip was edging precariously close to the truth and he knew it.

Ella raised her chin defiantly. "I didn't feel threatened, Philip."

Understanding blossomed across Philip's features.

"So, you called him specifically. Why has he not laid his claim?"

Ella narrowed her gaze. "Laid his claim? What are we? Animals?" She screwed up her face and pinched the bridge of her nose. "I mean, I know we're *kinda* animals. Oh, for fucksake." Exasperated, she dropped her hands to her side.

Stone trained his gaze on Philip and hoped he would take the hint to leave. She didn't need to learn this from an outsider.

Philip laughed heartedly. "You have much to learn about your new world, young one. I look forward to the awakening."

"Thanks," she muttered, making a face.

Philip flitted his dark eyes to Stone, then back to Ella. "You are also a white wolf, are you not?"

She swallowed hard and tipped her chin upward. "Yes."

He ran his index finger over his lower lip. "Interesting."

"Yes, totally fascinating," Ella nodded. She reached for her door handle. "However, my daughter is waiting for me, and the more we stand here, the more freaked out she's gonna get. I need to get going. It was nice to see you, Philip."

Without mixing any more words, she opened her door and got in.

Stone, on the other hand, remained where he was. If standing vigil would allow her the opportunity to leave unscathed, he'd be more than happy to do it.

Are you coming? Ella's thoughts broke through his own.

Go. I'll be right behind you. He responded, still keeping's eyes trained on Philip.

He sensed her approval as she slipped her vehicle into reverse.

When she had driven off, he stepped forward and allowed the growl he'd been holding back to unleash.

Philip chuckled, evidently amused. "She has no idea, does she?"

Stone snarled in response. The situation was anything but humorous to him. Ella had become an important piece of his life—more important than he could even describe. The last thing he needed was someone like Philip making light of it.

Philip dropped down until he rested his forearm across one bent knee. He looked Stone directly in the eyes and the intense power of an Alpha rolled off of him. Stone held his ground, regardless.

"You know, I'm not the only one with an eye for Ms. Ella. If you believe she is yours to claim, I suggest you don't waste time. Not everyone will be as...*understanding* as I am," Philip said, holding his gaze for a beat longer than necessary. "Let me assure you, if you don't, *I will.* She will need protection for what's coming."

Stone considered shifting back into his human

form so he could ask the questions hammering his brain.

For starters, what was coming? Secondly, how would claiming each other offer her more protection than she already had?

"You must know, moon wolves are rare," Philip said, standing up. He brushed off his knee and grinned. "To have two in the same pack—two who seem, perhaps, destined to be together... Well, let's just say, if that truly is the case, it could be *monumental.*"

Moon wolves?

Stone huffed an exhalation, unsure where Philip was going with this. He had never heard the term before—not in relationship to him or any other wolf.

But rather than saying anything else to Stone, power rose between the two of them, and Philip shifted into his enormous brown wolf. He stared long and hard at Stone, then with an ear-piercing howl, he ran off.

Confusion warred inside Stone's mind, but he didn't have the luxury of getting lost in it.

He turned around and ran after Ella.

CHAPTER 16
WHAT A MESS

ELLA

What in the blue blazes is going on?

Lay his claim?

I shake my head and sigh. The longer I'm a part of this supernatural world, the more strange things become. I really wish there was some sort of manual I could read so I wasn't constantly feeling like the dunce of the class.

"Mom, I really hate this," Avery says, pressing into her seat.

Surprised, I take my eyes off the road to glance in her direction. "Hate driving?"

"Funny," she says, making a face. "No, your new life. This *thing* going on with you. Whatever you wanna call it. I always feel like something is about to go horribly wrong. It's terrifying."

"Sweetie, I know it feels that way..."

"Because it *is* that way, Mom. We've been here for

a month and our lives have already been at risk half a dozen times," she squeaks.

"You're exaggerating—"

She holds up her hand and starts counting on her fingers. "When we nearly hit the white wolf—er, Stone. Then, witnessed the car wreck with Clementine's husband. The homicidal movers. The Silas guy that broke into our house and tried to—" she shudders, holding up four fingers. "At least you kicked his butt. Then, that gigantic guy and his crew of crazy women at the theater. Now, today. I feel like we can't even go somewhere *normal* without something nuts happening."

I reach out, extending my arm across the middle console with my palm face up. She eyes it, then places her hand inside mine.

"Honey, I know this has been mental. And it *really* has. It's a lot for all of us to adjust to. But the one thing I want you to know is that I will *always* protect you. No matter what. Got it?" I say, accidentally letting some of my newfound power entwine through my words.

There are times—like when I fiercely want to protect my own—that I can't help it. It just flows out.

Her eyes widen and she bites down on her lower lip. After a moment, she nods.

"Good," I say, squeezing her hand. "I can handle Philip. He's a good man, for the most part. Honorable, at least. And even if I couldn't deal with him alone, I have faith in the rest of the..." I narrow my gaze, still unsure how much of my new world my daughter can latch onto, "*group*. They would have my back."

"That's great for *your* back, but what about ours?" she asks, letting her gaze drift out the passenger window.

"You are both extensions of my back, numpty." I shoot her a lopsided grin.

She sighs heavily.

"Seriously, Avery. I won't let anything bad happen to you," I say, turning into our driveway. I put our Highlander into park and rotate to face her. "You and Asher are my world."

"It seems like your world is different now," she whispers.

"You might be right. Things are definitely different. But you have to remember, you're only a few years from being on your own, woman. Asher, even closer. Once you move out—"

"Once we're on our own it will be worse. At least living with you, I feel sorta safe."

"Honey," I say, trying to reassure her. "That's what I'm telling you. No matter where you go, you're protected. The Black Crater Pack is vast and we—"

She shakes her head. "It's not the same."

I drop my chin. "I know."

My insides flutter and I glance up to witness Stone's wolf trek across our lawn, then pad his way up the front porch stairs.

"Your boyfriend's here," Avery mutters.

"He's not my—" I pause, biting down on my lip. "I mean, I don't know what he is."

She nods, more to herself than to me, it seems. Then, without another word, she opens her car door and walks to the house. She doesn't stop or say hello to Stone. Instead, she just goes directly inside and closes the door behind her.

I let my head fall back to the headrest. "Shit."

If I'm not careful, I'm going to push her away. Avery's always been a sensitive soul and the divorce was enough of a big transition. I can only imagine how this is flipping her world upside down. As much as she could see Troy's behavior was toxic, she still loves her dad. So, even on a normal day, in a normal life—the idea of Mom dating someone new should be broached delicately.

Is everything okay? Stone asks through our mental connection.

I let out a slow breath. *I don't know, Stone. I honestly don't.*

Come out and talk to me.

I flit my gaze to him and nod. Then, I grab my purse and exit the Highlander.

He stands up as I get close and I wave him toward the house. "Come inside. We can talk in my bedroom."

I open the door and step aside. Stone's wolf trots past me and over to the bottom of the stairs. He waits briefly for me to catch up, then bolts up the staircase and chucks a right. He's in my bedroom before I even hit the top of the landing.

"Hi, Mom," Asher says, pulling his headset off his head. "Did you just get home?"

I nod. "Yup."

"Did you get your article finished?"

"Fuuuck," I groan, dropping my head back. I had forgotten all about the stupid article and my laptop that's sitting in the backseat.

He chuckles under his breath. "I'll take that as a *no*."

I return my gaze to him. "That's a no."

Without going into the details, I trudge past him and into my bedroom. By the time I get there, Stone is sitting on the edge of my bed, buck ass naked and glorious.

"You know, you should leave a change of clothes here," I mutter, fighting the insane tingle that reaches my nether regions.

I close the door behind me, just in case a kid decided to wander in and got an eyeful.

He quirks an eyebrow and a hint of a smirk brightens his face. "You want me to leave clothes here?"

I narrow my gaze. "You know what I mean."

"Do I?" His grin broadens and he stands up.

I zip my gaze to his emerald eyes and swallow hard. "You should, yes. Definitely."

Something inside me stirs, wanting desperately

not to talk—not to dress. Instead, it wants more than anything to feel his skin against mine.

"Ella, we need to talk about something," Stone says, all hint of playfulness vanishing before my eyes.

My heart sinks and my libido dampens. "Yeah, I think we do."

He raises a hand. "Ladies first."

I walk past him, sitting down on the edge of the bed. "Stone, I don't know how to do this. I feel like I'm messing it all up. The pack—they feel distant. Like they're no longer as sure about me as they were a month ago. To add to that uncertainty, I keep getting this feeling that I'm missing something important. Like, I'm screwing up the rules or something. Which, obviously I have been with the people I've been meeting. Only, I don't know what the rules are in the first place. And don't even get me started on how it's messing with Avery and Asher..."

My words tumble out and when I glance up, I half expect Stone to tell me I'm being ridiculous.

Instead, he kneels down in front of me, placing his hands on my knees. "Ella, the pack will be fine. They're only responding to your uncertainty. As soon as you get more settled, they will be, too. As for Avery and Asher..." he shakes his head, "I've never had kids. So I can only imagine how they're dealing with all of this."

"Avery is ready to melt down," I whisper, fighting back the tears prickling my eyes.

His lashes flutter against his cheeks and his lips

tug down slightly. "I'm sorry, Ella. I wish there was something I could do. Some way to take that for you."

"I just wish I could balance all of this better," I say.

"You're doing an incredible job. Anyone else would have lost their shit by now," Stone says, chuckling softly.

"Well, good thing I lost my shit a long time ago," I say, shrugging nonchalantly.

Part of me actually believes that. How else would you explain the way I've just rolled with these crazy punches?

He huffs a laugh. "Perhaps that does help."

"Stone, what did Philip mean back at the mall?" I say, staring deeply into his eyes. His pupils widen until they nearly swallow all of the green.

"Which part?" he asks, clearing his throat.

My eyebrows tug in and I say, "Claim... Philip said something about you laying your claim. What did he mean by that?"

Stone inhales sharply and stands up. I lean back on the bed, forcing my gaze to the ceiling, but it doesn't help. The intense urge returns and all I want to do is tear my own clothing off and screw his brains out.

What in the hell is wrong with me?

I clutch the blankets behind me, riding the wave until it starts to dissipate.

He sits down beside me and his voice is gruff when he says, "That's actually what I wanted to talk to you about."

I glance at him from the corner of my eye as he takes a deep, measured breath.

He scratches at the back of his head and snickers to himself. "You know, I don't even know how to start this."

"It can't be that hard," I say, regretting my choice of words the instant he glances at me and smirks.

God, it's like we're both sixteen.

I roll my hand between us, encouraging him to get moving. Goodness knows if I say anything else, it will just come out as innuendo.

"In werewolf packs, we aren't always in control of our relationships. Sometimes..." his voice trails off and he stares at the floor.

"Sometimes one dominates the other?" I ask, voicing the worry that's inhabited the back of my mind.

His eyes widen and he shakes his head. "No, that's not exactly—"

My phone rings, making me jump. You'd think with all of the new abilities I have, not getting startled by the phone when it rings could get added to the list.

"Hang on a sec," I say, holding up a finger. I extract my phone from my pocket and groan at the Caller ID.

It's Troy.

I hit ignore and set my phone down. No sense in answering that one. Nothing good can come from it, as I well know.

Stone's left eyebrow twitches in an obvious question.

I swipe a hand through the air. "It's just Troy. You were saying?"

He tilts his head in acknowledgment. "Well, humans have this saying—"

The phone rings again.

My expression deadpans and I force my breathing to go slow through my nostrils.

Seriously? What is his deal?

Again, I hold up a finger. "Hang on. Let me just deal with this or he'll keep hounding me until he gets his way." Stone stares at me, so I flick the phone on. "What do you want, Troy? I'm in the middle of something."

"I need you to book me a flight to Oregon," he says, apparently happy not to mince words.

"You want me to what? Are you high?" I scoff.

"I want to see the kids before school starts," Troy states matter-of-factly.

I shake my head, glancing at Stone. His expression is quizzical, but I ignore him for the moment and fire back, "And that's my problem how?"

"You always handled that stuff," Troy continues, as if that's the only explanation he needs.

Anger swells inside my chest and I bite back the insults I'd love to hurl in his direction.

"Well, no time like the present to figure out how it

works," I spit. "You're a big boy. If you want to visit your kids, you figure out how to make it happen."

I hang up the phone and shut it off completely. Hell, I should have just done that in the first place.

"You know what, Stone, I think you should go," I say rubbing the butt of my hand over my right eye.

I moved to Oregon to get away from Troy. Now he wants to visit?

Fuck my life.

As much as I enjoy Stone's presence and I want to understand this pack dynamic, right now I need to make sure I'm taking care of my responsibilities. The last thing I need is to get fired from my job.

Troy would have a field day.

"But I thought—" Stone begins.

"I know. We need to go further into this conversation, and we will, but the pack isn't my only responsibility. I need to get this article done and I've wasted enough time with pack duties this afternoon," I say, fighting the panic welling inside me.

The disappointment in his eyes is hard to miss. Yet, instead of speaking up about it, he simply nods and stands back up. "Okay."

"We can talk more about all of this at the party," I say, trying to sound happy and sincere when all I want to do is find something to punch.

CHAPTER 17

PART OF THE PACKAGE

ELLA

I f I could just get this stupid article sent off, I could finally relax, and maybe even enjoy the planning for the party tomorrow. But alas, the stupid thing is hanging around like a backache that just won't go away.

I don't know what the hell is wrong with me... It shouldn't be this hard to get the words out and send the article over to my boss.

I close the laptop and make my way downstairs. Clementine and Marta are nearly here, so there's no point in agonizing over it until they're gone.

When I get to the bottom of the stairs, I sense the two of them on my property, so I keep walking and open the front door. I have to admit, this ability to sense where pack members are does come in handy. It's like an internal app, keeping tabs on everyone.

Now, if only the same could be done for the kids

without turning them into supernatural beasts... That would be handy.

"Hey guys," I call out, raising my right hand and waving at them as they exit Marta's black sedan.

The fact that the two of them are willing to help me get this party under control is a total godsend. I don't know if I'd be able to do it all with work stuff stacked on top. I'd probably end up calling it off so I could hole myself up in my bedroom until the article was finished.

What kind of fun would that be?

I guess this is another privilege of being Alpha. Delegation is part of the package.

"Ready for tomorrow?" Clem asks, her green eyes flashing as walks up the stairs and onto the porch.

"If I was, I wouldn't need you two. Would I?" I snort.

"Girl has a point," Marta says, chuckling.

I wave them into the house. "Come on. We can grab drinks in the kitchen, then set up in the backyard. I need to get out of the house for a bit."

"Sounds good to me," Clementine says.

We walk down the hall to the kitchen, stopping only long enough for each of us to grab a glass of ice water. I snatch up the small notepad by the telephone and a pen from the junk drawer before leading them out to the backyard.

"Sorry, it's still kind of a mess. I was hoping to get more time to clean up back here," I say, setting down my water on the table. The glass table is covered with pollen and it's painfully evident I should have come out earlier to wipe things down.

"It's not a problem. Where are your paper towels?" Marta asks, turning back to the house.

I point from where I stand. "They're next to the sink. I think we might have some wet wipes there, too."

She nods and heads back inside.

"So, where are the kiddos?" Clementine asks with a smile as she takes her seat.

"Asher is turning applications in around town and Avery is upstairs in her room. Probably filming," I say, shooting her a knowing look. Whenever Avery is nowhere to be found, she's likely on TikTok.

Marta opens the back door with a bottle of wipes and paper towels in hand. "I come bearing cleaning supplies."

"Excellent," I say, grabbing the wipes and opening the lid.

They're probably overkill since they're the Clorox brand ones meant for mopping up kitchen goo, but they'll do. In a matter of minutes, the table is clean, clear, and ready for the party planning session at hand.

"Okay, so what's left to do?" Clementine asks, pulling out a ponytail holder and tying back her unruly brown hair. She puts it into one of those messy buns on the top of her head that I can never seem to manage.

I run my hand over my face. "All of it?"

Marta laughs. "Told you."

"Seriously, guys. I know I'm the one who wanted to do this thing—and I definitely still do—it's just that this article is driving me bonkers," I mutter, floating my gaze around the backyard. The grass hasn't even been mowed and while the rest of the yard looks decent, it will still need to be done before the party.

Looks like a job for Asher this afternoon.

"Don't let the party stress you out. We'll do whatever we can to help out, so it's a no-pressure kind of thing. Besides, it's just meant to be a fun, 'get to know you' kind of event. Right?" Clementine asks.

I nod. "Yeah. I mean, there are pack members I haven't even met yet. And I feel like, in order to make an impact here, everyone has to kinda be on the same page. You know?"

The two of them nod in unison.

"Plus, it will help me to put faces to the feelings I get. I have to admit, it's a little weird sensing people but not even knowing who they are," I say, scrunching my face. "When I was first... I don't know, *anointed* or whatever, I got this deep sense of belonging and pride. Like everyone was happy I was here. Now it just sorta feels like there's confusion or listlessness."

Marta nods. Her golden hair flutters in the breeze,

but since it's cut so short, she doesn't have the same issues keeping it at bay as Clementine.

"I believe you are right. The pack will feel more settled after getting to know you and your family," she says.

"That's the plan," I say, allowing a slow smile to creep upon my face. "I'm hopeful that my kids will feel a bit more...*settled,* as well. The Portland Pack has really done a number on Avery. Her anxiety is through the roof."

"Poor kid. I can only imagine," Clem says, her lips tugging downward. "They've been through a lot."

I lift my eyebrows in agreement. "Well, anyway, enough of my pity party. We need to swap to the *actual* party," I mutter, reaching out and tapping the pen on the notepad. "In my head, the only thing we really need to plan out is the menu and the fireworks. I don't plan on decorating or anything."

"Where do you intend on holding this party?" Marta asks, her gaze sweeping over the backyard.

I shrug sheepishly. "Well, I *was* thinking here."

They both exchange a significant glance.

"What? Is it too—"

"Small? Yes," Marta snickers.

"Really?" I say, scrunching my face.

"Oh yeah," Clementine says, nodding in agreement. "If everyone stopped in, you'd be overrun. You need a place with a bit more space."

"Well, shit," I say, leaning back in my chair. "Then where? It's a little late to contact a park, isn't it?"

"What about Stone's?" Marta asks, flitting her gaze to Clementine. "He has quite a bit of land. Plus, it would make sense, all things considered."

I catch a whiff of something unsaid going between Marta and Clementine and I quirk an eyebrow. When neither of them makes a move to clue me in, I cross my arms over my chest. "And what exactly does that mean?"

Marta clears her throat. "Simply that it would be a gesture of support that further embraces Stone back into the pack."

"Yeah, and the fact that you're shagging my brother." Clementine snickers.

My mouth gapes open. "Okay, so first of all, I'm not shagging Stone."

"*Yet*," Clementine corrects.

I narrow my gaze and huff a sigh. "Yet."

"But you will be. Anyone with eyeballs can see it. This means, the likelihood of the two of you becoming," Clementine's face screws up, "*a thing* is highly probable. Thus, his place makes just as much sense as yours."

"Do you think he'll be okay with having the party at his place?" I ask.

Clem swipes a hand in the air. "Eh, he'll be fine."

"Having the party at his place would also make it

easier for pack members to come and go in whatever form they choose," Marta interjects.

Clementine nods.

"Oh, god. They're not going to be wandering the party naked. Are they?" I say, suddenly getting visions of nude people galavanting all over the place. "That would freak the kids right out. I mean, me too, if I'm honest."

Marta laughs and Clementine nearly spits out her water.

Clem wipes her mouth with the back of her hand. "We can warn them that clothing *is* required."

I breathe a sigh of relief. "Okay, cool."

"I'll make sure we're all good with Stone and that the pack knows where to meet. Are we doing an end-of-the-day kind of deal? Like supper to sundown?" Clementine asks, back to serious.

I nod. "Yeah, that'll work."

"Allow me to take care of the meal arrangements. I can get a few others involved to help," Marta says.

"Okay, great. What do I do?" I laugh.

The party is no longer at my place and from the sounds of things, the rest of the arrangements are going to take care of themselves.

I could get used to this.

"You and Stone could figure out the fireworks," Clem says, wiggling her eyebrows suggestively.

I glare at her. "Why do I get the impression you're

not talking about the bright lights that actually get shot off in the sky?"

"Oh, those, too," she says with a wink.

I shake my head, trying not to laugh. For being Stone's sibling, she sure is more than happy to push us together. She reminds me so much of Denise. I bet the two of them would have a field day together.

I drop my pen and take a sip of water. If only my article came together as easily as this. Then I wouldn't be nearly as stressed out.

"Ella, I have a feeling, things are going to change for the better here," Marta says, leaning back in her chair and sighing contently.

"It wasn't *that* terrible before," Clem cuts in, shooting Marta a look of consternation.

"No, that's true. But as great as Doug was," Marta says, clearly stepping gingerly with Clementine here, "his alliance with Silas did create a rift in the pack."

"That's fair." Clementine nods. "Doug tried hard to do the right thing by everyone. Unfortunately, the right thing would have been to oust Silas."

I shake my head. "I still don't understand what happened there. Why would Doug allow Silas to be Beta and outcast Stone?"

Marta and Clementine exchange another significant glance.

"What is it?" I ask, practically holding my breath.

"It is probably best for Stone to be the one to discuss that with you," Marta says, lowering her voice.

I glance between the two of them, wondering what it is they're hiding. "Well, he has...*sorta*. He was a bit cryptic at the time, though."

The two of them nod as if that makes perfect sense.

I lower my eyebrows and practically pout. "This isn't fair, guys. Don't make me bust out my Alpha voice."

Clementine laughs again and points in my direction. "Look at her. Only Alpha for a month and already abusing her power."

"Hey, I didn't actually *do* it."

"True." Clem nods. "Oh, go on and tell her, Marta. Stone's not gonna want to explain this one."

Marta's golden eyes widen and she inhales sharply. "Ella, you must understand... There are rules each pack goes by in order to maintain peace and tranquility."

"Of course," I say, leaning in a bit, enthralled by the sudden history lesson and the possibility of learning more about Stone's past.

Marta nods, picking up her glass and taking a sip of water. "With our pack—and with most, actually—it goes against our laws to kill a human."

My stomach clenches and I hold my breath.

She takes a deep breath. "Well, Stone was outcast because—"

"Mom, your cellphone keeps going off, so I answered it," Avery says, as she opens the door and extends her arm out. In her hand is my cellphone.

"I'm busy, Avery," I say, shaking my head.

Her brown eyes widen and she thrusts the phone at me a second time. "I answered it for you. It's your boss."

"Shit," I mutter under my breath as I kick my chair back and stand up.

Avery passes the phone over to me, waves quickly at the two women beside me, then rushes back into the house.

I clutch the phone to my chest for a moment, trying to work through what I can tell him that will keep him happy.

Both Marta and Clementine look apprehensive but neither of them says a word.

I inhale deeply, then bring the phone to my ear. "Hey, Matt. How are you doing?"

"Good. I'm doing good. Look, Ella, we need to have a talk," Matt begins. His tone is all business and my heart sinks before he even speaks his next words. "I'm sure this isn't going to come to any huge surprise, considering the past couple of weeks. I wish this was in person..."

"What is it?" I ask, holding my breath.

"Ella, I'm afraid we're going to have to let you go."

CHAPTER 18
PRE-PARTY CHAOS

ELLA

I fucking knew it.

My heart rate increases as I stare at my bedroom ceiling and replay the call over and over again in my mind.

Fired.

Matt was right. I did see this coming.

However, I had hoped he'd give me more time. Or that he'd cut me a little slack. It's not like things have been a walk in the park this year. Besides, I've always been a good writer for them.

What in the hell am I going to do now?

I close my eyes and groan.

Money is kinda necessary and goodness knows I get fuck-all from Troy for child support. That was part of the divorce deal. I get the kids, he gets to galavant off into the sunset without supporting them at all. Well, not very far, anyway. I can barely keep groceries for a day in the house for the paltry sixty dollars he sends each month.

While I have to admit, the relief of no longer having to write that article is real—because let's face it, I didn't want to write it. Unfortunately, it's like a huge weight has been lifted off my shoulders only to be pressed on my chest instead.

God, I wish this gig with the pack paid. That would make my life a helluva lot easier. Especially since it's consuming so much of my mind and time.

It's just like me to pick up a massive new responsibility that doesn't even support me. It's like I'm attracted to getting shafted. And *not* in a good way.

My thoughts flit to Stone and the strange conversations I've been having lately.

Did Stone kill someone? Is that why he was cast out?

If so, he sure left that out of the conversation.

I'm not sure how I feel about it, either. Part of me is like...*typical guy.* The other part is still totally cool with him.

How twisted is that?

I wonder if I can ask him before the party tonight. I'd rather settle my mind sooner rather than later since Clementine and Marta made a run for it as soon as they found out I was fired.

If I get moving, I could be at his place early under the guise of setting up.

Agitation forces me to sit up in bed. Sighing to myself, I get out and walk over to my dresser. I pluck out a bra, capris, and a tank top for the day and shimmy into them. No point lingering in bed when there's so much to do. There's no time like the present to get my ass in gear.

It's barely gone seven in the morning, so there's no chance either of the kids will be up yet. I trudge past their closed doors and pad my way down the stairs in search of coffee.

When I get to the kitchen, I prep the coffee maker and turn it on. The sound of beans grinding bursts into the space and I walk over to the sink to get a glass of water while I wait.

My gaze extends out the kitchen window into the backyard and I sigh to myself.

The grass still needs to be mowed.

What a mess.

I slam the contents of my water and spin on my heel. "Come on, Ella. Get a grip. You're resourceful and have plenty of skills. You got this. Today, focus on the party. Tomorrow, hunt for a new job."

Shaking my head, I dig through the cupboard and grab my travel mug so I can take my coffee to go. If I've gotta get the fireworks for tonight, I may as well do it now before the place is overrun.

Besides, then I can corner Stone with plenty of time to spare.

Within a few minutes, I have my coffee in hand

and texts sent to the kids so they know where I am going. Then, I lock up and head to the Highlander.

The birds are singing and the sun is shining as I meander the sidewalk to my vehicle. I inhale the scents of summer and let it wash away some of my anxiety.

Yet, the moment I sit down in the vehicle, a different energy takes over.

I've been so busy with other things, I haven't given any thought to the pack. Or how this party will go. A couple of weeks ago, it was the most important thing on my mind. Now, it's barely even registered on the list of things to obsess over.

What if they don't like us? Will it be hard to win them over now that the fight with Silas is in the past?

I put the vehicle in reverse, letting the worries tumble around in my head.

To avoid letting my thoughts spiral out of control, I turn on my radio and crank my *Kickass Motivation Playlist*. It always helps me shift my vibe and look at things differently.

By the time I reach the large circus-like tent at the far end of the grocery store parking lot, I'm feeling much better. Granted, the tent is already buzzing with people going in and out with their arms full of boxes with fireworks.

The men, of course, walk out with armfuls of the most giant fireworks known to man. The things are so massive, that they're practically the size of their heads.

Compensating for something else, perhaps?

I snicker under my breath and keep walking.

The women seem to be walking out with the smaller multi-box sets and sparklers. *Go figure.*

"Ella? Hey, Ella, wait up," someone calls over my right shoulder.

I turn around, surprised to see Jinx waving a hand in the air and half-jogging, half-hobbling in my direction.

I wave back and stop moving so she can catch up.

Jinx would be hard to miss, even if she wasn't waving like a lunatic. Her flaming red and orange hair catches the sunlight in ways that truly look like it's on fire. For the briefest of moments, I have to wonder if it's a demon thing, or if she dyes her hair like the rest of us.

"Thanks," she says when she catches up. She bends over, catching her breath.

"Hey, Jinx. What are you doing here?" I ask, realizing it's nice to see a friendly face.

"Oh, you know..." She clutches at her chest, still trying to breathe. Finally, she stands up a bit straighter and says, "Wreaking havoc and pandemonium."

As if on cue, a car behind her backs out of a parking space and into the front bumper of another.

My fingertips fly to my mouth but she doesn't even flinch.

"So, what about you? Getting fireworks?" Jinx asks, tipping her chin to the tent.

I drop my hands, tearing my eyes away from the scene unfolding as the drivers exit their vehicles in what looks like a proper fight. I nod. "Yeah, I'm having a Fourth of July party."

As soon as the words come out, I feel like an ass for not inviting her. However, I know that wouldn't go down well. If I turned up with a Chaos Demon, I'm pretty sure the pack would disown me and request Silas to come back.

"Me, too," she grins, pointing back toward the grocery store, "I was just getting some last-minute goodies."

"You celebrate the Fourth?" I ask, genuinely surprised. If the pack doesn't care about things like the Fourth of July, I wouldn't have thought she would.

She snickers. "Why wouldn't I?"

I shake my head. "No reason. I mean, I guess I figured..." I stop talking before I have to put my foot in my mouth.

She bends in, a twinkle of mischievousness in her eyes. "Do you know how much chaos I can cause on a night like this without drawing too much attention to myself? It's *glorious*."

My eyes widen at the prospect. And the fact that she basically flat out admitted what she is to me.

"Yeah, I suppose that would be—" I begin, not quite sure what to say to something like that.

"So, whatcha getting? Have you decided yet?" Jinx asks, jabbing a finger toward the fireworks tent.

I shrug. "I have absolutely no idea. My only requirement is nothing that could blow up my son's hand if he gets ahold of a lighter."

Jinx laughs heartedly, clutching at her side. "Yeah, boys have a way of flirting with danger, don't they? I love them so much. They're an easy mark, let me tell you."

Despite myself, I chuckle. "I can imagine, actually. Two guys just left with enough fireworks to blow up their houses."

Her eyes light with excitement. "Oooh, now that's a good idea. I could work with that."

"Jinx, oh my god," I say, covering my mouth and shaking my head. However, the thought of one of these guys with a hoard of rocket launcher-style fireworks getting a big surprise is pretty funny.

As long as I'm far, far away from it.

She steps forward, nudging me with her shoulder. "See, I knew there was something different about you. You're not like the rest of those snooty howlers."

"How'd you—"

She narrows her eyes and lowers her voice to barely a whisper. "I have a kind of *tuner*, I guess you could say, It alerts me to the energies around me and helps me to be more effective."

My eyebrows rise of their own accord. "Oh."

It actually makes total sense.

She winks at me and pats me on the arm like I'm a child just learning how to walk. "Well, have to talk soon. I can tell you more about my nature if that's what you want. Besides, there's something I want to discuss with you. Unfortunately, I need to get back to the house right now. Otherwise, the ice is going to melt and my guests will flip their shit. Talk soon?"

I nod. "Sure, that sounds good."

"Excellent," Jinx says, and a big, goofy grin spreads across her hips. "Later." She pauses for a beat, then turns to walk away.

She only manages a few feet before shouting erupts behind me.

I turn to face the fireworks tent just as a man carrying one of those big ass fireworks exits. His eyes just about bug out of his head as the thing bursts into flames in his hands. Then, with a loud bang, it shoots out of the box and into the corner of the tent. The thing bounces off the metal post, shooting colorful flames in all directions.

Two women in the tent drop everything in their arms and make a run for it. Another guy just stands in the center, eyes wide, and ready to go down in flames if the rest of it ignites.

The sales guy at the counter drops the credit card machine and scrambles from behind his podium. He races to the corner, trying to kick the other boxes clear of the showering flames.

Unfortunately, one of the smaller ones kicks off, sending fountains of light shooting from even smaller boxes beside him.

He squeals like a little kid, turns around abruptly, and races for a fire extinguisher behind the podium.

Not a single person makes a move to help him. Myself, included. We all just stand there in complete, dumbfounded awe.

I'd have to stifle a laugh if I wasn't enthralled in the display of utter chaos happening before my eyes.

The guy trips on his way back with the fire extinguisher, knocking a display rack to the ground and sending the extinguisher flying across the space.

Suddenly, the guy who lost his rocket launcher of a firework is on the move. He races forward, grabbing the extinguisher, and letting it rip.

Before I know it, the entire front left corner of the tent, and all of the contents in the vicinity are covered in white goo. But thankfully, the rest of the fireworks seem to be safe.

For now.

Good lord, that woman *does* wreak havoc and pandemonium wherever she goes.

Trying desperately not to laugh, I shake my head and turn to watch Jinx hobble her way to her vehicle with *almost* everyone around her none the wiser.

CHAPTER 19
SECRETS REVEALED

ELLA

B y the time I pull into Stone's driveway, I'm feeling a helluva lot better.

I don't know what it is about Jinx. Maybe it's the way she can revel in the chaos all around her. Either way, I love her no-fucks-given attitude.

I wanna be her when I grow up.

My life might be one giant hot mess right now and the more I can embrace the chaos and still find beauty, the better off I'll be.

I put the Highlander into park and glance around Stone's property. Clementine and Marta were right, this is a much better location for the party. Not only is the house bigger, but the yard is, as well. There are large willow trees in the back and plenty of lawn space to meander around and chat.

Plus, it's a much safer location to set off the small fortune I spent on fireworks.

Before I get out of the vehicle, I grab my phone and text the kids, letting them know I'll be back this afternoon to get them. I'm sure they'll be thrilled since I had originally told them they'd be helping get the party set up.

Clutching the phone in my left hand, I exit the vehicle and walk toward Stone's modest-size house. As I get closer, I slow down a bit, taking more of the building's features in.

The last time I was here, it was pitch black, and truth be told, I was more focused on not staring at Stone's naked butt as he went inside to get a change of clothes.

Of course, that was an epic fail. He has a *nice* ass.

The gray siding and multi-colored stone lower half definitely look like something he'd choose. How I know that is beyond me. Maybe it's because it's almost as if the house is a billboard for its owner.

I glance around at the landscaping near the house. He doesn't have much in the way of gardens, but the yard looks nice enough, and the driveway is certainly capable of taking on a bunch of cars.

Granted, I doubt many of them will arrive that way, come to think of it.

My eyes widen and I suck in a breath.

God, I hope Clementine spread the *clothing* is *required* rule.

Exhaling loudly, I make my way to the front door and knock.

I can tell he's at home from the low hum that throbs from the center of my chest.

It takes him a few minutes to come to the door, but when he does, he's clad in a pair of sleep pants...*and nothing else*. Even his feet are bare.

His dark hair is disheveled, giving him a rugged appearance that makes my insides flutter.

And oh, those tattoos...

I sweep my gaze across his chest and arms, loving everything I'm seeing. It sets things ablaze that haven't been ablaze for decades. And again, I instantly flashback to the other day.

"Sorry, Ella. Did I know you were coming so early?" he asks, running a hand through his hair and yawning.

I shake my head, checking my watch. It's just past ten in the morning. "No, it was kind of an impromptu thing. Mind if I come in?"

"Not at all," he says, stepping back and opening the door wider for me.

"Thanks." I make my way inside, inhaling deeply the scent I've come to know as uniquely his.

The entryway envelops a person in a sort of warm hug. It has dark, mahogany-colored wood paneling and ironworks as embellishments on all the light fixtures and the staircase railings to the right.

A dorky smile creeps across my face and my shoulders relax a bit.

Stone walks past me, waving for me to follow him.

He turns left, entering a large kitchen and dining area combo.

"Thanks for agreeing to have the party here," I say, inspecting the kitchen with intense curiosity. "You have a nice place."

He glances over to me, blinking back what I can only assume is grogginess. "Oh, right. I forgot you didn't come in last time. Did you?"

I press my lips tight and shake my head.

"Do you want some coffee?" he asks, pointing to the coffee maker and shifting closer to it.

"I'd love some."

The coffee I had brought with me is still in the Highlander, completely untouched. With all of the commotion at the fireworks place, it completely slipped my mind.

He nods, setting to work and humming as he does so.

I love how his kitchen is laid out. There are big stainless steel appliances and dark granite countertops laid over deep brown cabinets. The floor is kind of a slate tile that looks like it should be part of a castle more than a kitchen. But what I love most is that there are plenty of windows, each overlooking a different vantage point of his woods. There isn't a single neighbor in sight.

"You're very secluded out here," I say, admiring the view from the large picture window off to the left of the two-person dining table.

"I like it." He pours two cups of coffee and meanders over to the table. "So, is everything okay?"

I turn back to him and nod absently. "Yeah, fine." But as soon as I say the words, my face crumples. Now's not the time for lies. If I want him to open up, I need to be vulnerable, too. "Actually, that's a lie," I whisper, taking a seat at the table.

"What's up?" He sits down opposite me, his expression darkening as he surveys my every move.

My forehead creases with the thoughts pinging around in my brain and fighting for attention. Finally, I say, "I'm going to get straight to the point, so don't be offended. Okay?"

His eyebrows knit together. "Okay."

I clear my throat, steeling myself for a moment before saying, "Did you kill someone?"

Stone chokes slightly on his sip of coffee. "What?"

"Is that why Doug cast you out?" I press, trying to will my hammering heart back into my chest. This is the last thing I want to be asking, but I need to know.

"Who told you this?" he asks, setting his cup back down and tapping its edge.

I bite down on my lower lip. "It's not so much as what anyone said. More what I'm sensing. I just want to understand things, Stone. I don't have the luxury of being a part of this world my whole life. I need to lean on what I do best and *ask questions.*"

He nods, staring at his cup. "Well, I'm not a huge

fan of revisiting the past, but for you, I'll make an exception."

His green eyes flit upward, locking onto mine.

"Okay," I whisper.

"Just promise me something," he says, exhaling slowly.

"Anything."

He holds my gaze, then nods. "If this changes anything between you and me—" His voice cracks slightly and he clears his throat. "If you have second thoughts about *anything*, just say so right away. Don't wait and let things fester."

I steel my breath.

Shit, this must be really bad.

Rather than letting my voice betray me, I just tip my head in agreement.

"Silas had always had ambitions. Even when we were younger. He wanted to one day take over the pack or have his own. But everyone could see that his desires weren't for the greater good. He only cared about power," Stone says, again dropping his gaze to his cup. "No one knew that more than me. He had made false claims a number of times, trying to get the pack to turn against me. He knew that I was the key to ascending, so to speak. It never worked, though. The pack could sense his dishonesty and without proof—"

Stone suddenly stands up, the muscles across his chest flexing with his clenched fists.

"What did he do?" I press.

Stone's jaw quivers. "He *created* proof."

Pain rolls off of him and even if I wasn't connected to him through this pack connection, it's clear in his very demeanor.

I stand up, making my way to him. Reaching out, I press my hand to his upper arm. "What happened?"

His dark eyebrows lower and he stares hard at me for a moment. "He sent a human to attack me. I'd been stupid—drinking at a human bar downtown after work. I wasn't even fully in my right mind if I'm honest."

A wave of guilt passes from Stone and through me.

"I was getting ready to shift in the alley when this guy came out of nowhere. He started spouting off stupid shit about me. How I looked, the way I was dressed. The fact I was drinking alone. None of it mattered. I've never given a shit about what people think of me. But then he attacked me with a knife. It was so unexpected—and I'd been drinking, so I wasn't thinking properly. I went into defensive mode and pushed him off me," his voice trails off and he runs a hand through his hair. His eyes close and he sighs, "I pushed him too hard. Didn't even try to dampen my strength. He slammed into the brick building behind him. His skull split open like a cantaloupe."

I shudder from the imagery, but whisper, "Stone, it wasn't your fault."

He chuckles darkly. "It didn't matter. Silas got what he wanted. I found out later that he'd paid the guy to jump me. He'd also paid someone else to film the whole thing. So, naturally, when others saw the footage…"

"They had to make an example of you," I say, realization settling in. "That's why Doug did what he did. There was veritable proof and he couldn't just sweep it under the rug."

Stone nods, anguish flitting through his features.

Relief floods through me. There's no question in my mind—or my being—that Stone is telling the truth. In fact, it all makes perfect sense now, based on everything I've come to know of his character.

I reach out, sliding my right hand into his left. "Thank you for telling me."

His lashes flutter against his cheeks but he doesn't say anything.

"And for the record, I'm not changing my mind," I whisper, feeling the heat spread from our palms to the rest of my body.

The intensity in Stone's eyes deepens and relief flashes across his face. "You have no idea how happy I am to hear that."

I squeeze his hand. "For what it's worth, Doug knew it was bullshit, too."

"How would you know that?" Stone snickers.

"Because I can feel the authenticity of your story," I say. "If I can, he did, too."

He nods, letting a faint smile break through the darkness of his expression.

I inhale sharply and point back to the table. "Now that we're clear there, I have another question, but I'm sure it won't be anywhere near as charged. But first, our coffee is getting cold and I hate drinking cold coffee."

I want to get an understanding of what Philip had said the other day now that we have the time to get into it. It feels like it could be another important piece to the puzzle.

However, as soon as the words come out, I sense Clementine in the vicinity. Stone must sense her, too, because he glances over his shoulder, looking out the window that faces the driveway.

"Clementine is on her way," Stone says.

"Yeah, I caught that," I say, nodding. "Shit. Maybe it should wait."

He narrows his eyes. "You sure?"

I swipe a hand in the air. "Yeah, it's not like it's going anywhere. We can talk about it tomorrow."

Before Stone can respond, Clementine opens the front door and calls out, "It's party time, bitches!"

CHAPTER 20

QUITE THE SHINDIG

STONE

Stone felt like a huge weight had been lifted from his shoulders.

Having to tell Ella the story about his banishment had been weighing on his mind since the moment he realized what Doug had done to her.

He desperately wanted her to see him as a man of honor. Not someone who was prone to losing control.

Now that she knew, and it didn't even faze her, it freed his mind up for other possibilities—like the very thing she had wanted to discuss before Clementine arrived.

The conversation about fated mates and the claiming process wasn't only on her mind. It was on his, as well. He wanted to open the discussion and lay it all out on the line. However, he wasn't sure how she'd feel about any of it.

One thing was certain, after having the more difficult conversation, he no longer feared what she might do or say.

Hell, that conversation might even go well, too.

And if it did...

His wolf somersaulted at the idea.

If he was really honest with himself, he wanted it all to be true. He wanted to be destined for her.

The repercussions of such an idea expanded far beyond what Stone could ponder at the present moment.

Stone watched her from the backyard as she and Clementine flitted from place to place, setting things up for the party. She already fit in here, in his big backyard. It was almost as if it was her own home, as well.

He liked the feeling of that more than he would have dared to admit.

Once this party was over, Stone promised himself he would tell her how he felt. He had kept his distance long enough. He would explain everything and let her steer the direction they traveled next.

Besides, he would be damned if he didn't heed Philip's warning. He wasn't that naive.

"Marta," Ella beamed, waving.

Stone stopped tinkering with the party tent Clem insisted upon and glanced over his shoulder to find the pack's new Beta stepping from the sidewalk and onto the grass.

"Wow, Stone's place sure does clean up nice," Marta said as she eyed the twinkling lights that now hung from the tree branches and the tables that had been set out by Ella and Clementine.

"Are you kidding? It was a perfect clean slate to make magic happen," Ella said, rubbing her hands together. "Now, I just need to grab my kids before everyone arrives. Then we'll be set for blast off."

"I can get them," Clementine said, swiping a hand in the air. "Sit. Stay. *Relax*."

"Are you sure?" Ella said, surprise evident in the way her forehead creased. She wasn't used to people helping her.

A pang of sorrow swept through him. She deserved so much more than what she had been given.

"Sit," Clem repeated, giving Ella a knowing look. Then, she turned around and made her way to the front of the house.

Stone finished tying down the tent and walked over to Marta and Ella.

The rest of the pack would be arriving soon. Stone could sense many of them already heading their way.

"Can you believe her?" Ella chuckled to Marta. "She's been nonstop since she got here and she still wants to go pick up my kids. That woman is either nuts or a godsend."

"As her brother, I will opt for the former," Stone chuckled as he approached.

Ella grinned, gently slapping his upper arm with the back of her hand. "You don't count."

He shrugged. "I *have* known her longest."

Instead of responding, Ella just smiled bigger and shook her head.

"What else do you want done?" Stone asked.

She glanced around. "Nothing. I think we're good to go. Don't you?"

"It looks great," Marta said, nodding in agreement. "Festive."

"Before the rest of the pack arrives, did we have anything we need to announce or go over?" Stone asked, opening the cooler and grabbing a bottle of ice water. He held one out to Marta and Ella, as well.

"Oh, yes, I wondered the same—" Marta began. She took Stone's offering and muttered her appreciation.

Ella shook her head. "Okay, first of all, water is for pansies. I'm having a hard lemonade. It's been a long day." She pointed at the cooler to the left. "Secondly, guys, this is a *party*. Not a pack meeting. The only rule here tonight is *to have fun*. No shop talk, for crying out loud. Just good old-fashioned getting to know each other better."

Stone dug into the second cooler and handed Ella a bottle of hard lemonade.

"You're an angel." She took it with a goofy grin and sat down in one of the lawn chairs.

"So, we just...*sit*? And drink?" Marta asked, taking a seat beside her.

Ella cracked open her bottle and rolled her eyes. "Yeesh, you guys don't do fun much, do you? Oh, look,

Seth's here." She waved from her chair, then took a swig from her bottle.

Stone turned to glance over his shoulder.

Seth wasn't alone. Ramsey and Dina's family, as well as Bryce, followed right behind him. As did a number of other pack members.

Ready or not, it appeared the party had officially started.

By the time Stone looked back, Ella was on her feet. She made her way to the newcomers, introducing herself and getting to know a little bit about each of them.

He had to marvel at the effortlessness with which she flitted from person to person, making sure they had what they wanted and knew they could connect with her at any time.

She was by far, the most accessible Alpha he'd ever had the privilege of working with. Hell, *of knowing.*

More often than not, the Alpha stayed secluded, wanting to lead their pack with an iron fist or the declarations from high. It was clear to him, and likely the rest of the pack, that she was no ordinary Alpha.

It filled him with pride to know he'd somehow been sucked into her vortex of influence. After all the years alone, he had resigned himself to always being on the outside.

And now, a whole new world was opening up to him.

Within minutes, the backyard was filled with the

sounds of kids laughing and squealing as they played games and chased one another from one end of the yard to the other. Adults broke off into smaller groups, talking amongst themselves with food and drinks in hand.

Instantly, the energy was laid back and relaxed. Exactly the vibe he knew Ella was going for.

When Clementine made it back with Ella's kids, Stone fired up the grill to get the brats and burgers going.

While he had reservations at first, Stone had to admit that Ella's plan for hosting this party may have been exactly what they all needed. Not only were they connecting more with her and her kids—the pack itself was connecting more with each other, as well.

It was astounding to witness.

They had always been a cohesive unit, but looking back, it had been more functional than anything else.

Stone was impressed as the afternoon went off without a hitch. Everyone seemed to genuinely have a good time.

"Did you see? Asher's making friends," Ella whispered under her breath as she came up beside Stone. When he turned to see what she meant, she clutched his arm tight. "Don't stare—"

Stone chuckled and focused his other senses to understand what she was describing. Asher was in conversation by the fire pit with Penelope's daughter,

Cora. He couldn't help but smile. Cora was a second-generation wolf but she'd never really jived with anyone in the pack. There weren't many who were close in age. They were either a year or two younger or older.

"He seems like a good fit for her," Stone said from the side of his mouth.

"Is she nice?" Ella's response came feverishly.

He nodded. "Very. Cora's a sweet girl. Have you met Penelope yet?" He pointed to the food tent.

"Yes, she's a sweetheart." Ella nodded. "She was the first of her family to be born with the werewolf gene. Oh... She's Cora's mom?"

Stone chuckled. "Yes."

She removed her hand from his arm and strummed her fingertips together. "Hmmm... Now I must recon." Ella rubbed her hand over his back, causing him to shiver under her touch. "I'll be back."

She bound away, heading straight for Penelope.

"You look happy," Clementine said, approaching from the middle of the yard.

"Hmph," he muttered, feigning indifference.

"Oh, don't you start that bullshit. This life suits you," Clem responded.

She stepped onto the patio, eyeing the platters of food he'd already cooked. She picked up one of the smaller brats and took a bite.

Stone didn't know what to say to any of that. He was just happy to see everyone else so happy.

Clementine's deliberate stare made him self-conscious but he continued to work the grill.

"You should go hang out with Ella. Introduce her to some of the other pack members," Clem said. "I can take over here."

"She's doing a fine job on her own."

"Yes, but I have a feeling she'd like you by her side." Clementine shrugged, pulling a ponytail holder from her pocket. She tied her hair back into an unruly ponytail and shooed him aside.

Stone shook his head but allowed her to take over without much fight. It would be nice to step away and be a part of the fray. He handed her the spatula and backed away with his hands up.

"Yes, that's right. Be gone," she said, accepting the spatula and eyeing what was already on the grill.

"Thanks, Clem," he said.

She grinned broadly but there was a hint of sadness hidden in those green eyes of hers. He knew all too well that keeping busy was her way of coping. It was a trait they both shared.

A few months ago, she was the Alpha's mate and the pack dynamic was vastly different.

It was a wonder how she had been able to bounce back the way she had.

She was a strong woman, that was for certain.

Stone meandered toward Ella but was intercepted by Avery.

"Do you know when we're going to do the fireworks?" she asked, her face alight with giddy anticipation.

The sun was setting but it wasn't quite dark enough for fireworks yet. The daylight sensors had turned on the twinkle lights, though, so it wouldn't be long before they could set them off.

"Give it a half hour or so," he said with a wink.

Avery clapped, then pranced away to return to a small grouping of teen girls. She, too, had made friends it seemed.

Stone smiled as they began to chatter away about the photos and video shots they wanted to take.

By the time he reached Ella, she had gone from speaking only with Penelope to having a small group gathered around her, as well. Like mother, like daughter.

He took up residence beside her, observing the group. As she spoke and interacted with each of them, he felt the bond between the pack grow stronger. It was like the webbing that connected each of them was renewing—weaving together in new, more dynamic ways.

If Ella noticed it, she hadn't let on. But she was certainly more happy than he'd seen her in days. She was practically glowing.

The full moon had begun to rise, adding a level of connection and power to the pack. It tugged at his animal, enticing it to rise so he could run through the forest.

When the party was over, he'd ask Ella if she'd like to join him. He hadn't seen Ella's wolf since last month and something inside him wanted to witness its glory again.

"What do you think, Stone?"

He blinked, realizing someone had said his name. "I'm sorry, what?"

"Where were you just now?" Ella laughed.

He shook his head and focused on her. "Sorry, zoned out there for a minute. What did you say?"

"Penelope and I were wondering if it's time to start the fireworks. Better we start it so the teens don't get restless, if you know what I mean," she said, pressing her lips tight and squinting one of her eyes.

"A fair point. Yes, let's get it underway," he said, getting up and meandering over to the fireworks setup.

"Who's ready for fireworks?" Ella called out, urging everyone to follow her. "Come on. Fireworks!"

Avery's group was up and on the move the moment the words had escaped Ella's mouth.

The rest of the pack filed in behind, sitting down on the grass or parking themselves in the folding chairs scattered around the yard. How they managed to get the seventy-odd people to corral at the same time, he'd never know.

Ella walked up to him and whispered, "You got this?"

He nodded. "I think I can handle it."

She beamed at him and sat down in the front row sitting between Asher and Avery's groups.

Stone started with the fountain fireworks. They were the least crazy, but a good starter firework that would get the kids excited for more. He moved on to some of the medium fireworks until only the largest remained.

"Do we want one at a time? Or a big finale?" Stone called out enjoying the energy of the pack. It was a heightened experience that overrode everything.

"Finale!" the kids called out in unison.

Even some of the adults echoed the sentiment.

He shook his head and chuckled under his breath. "Finale it is. Be ready."

The laughter and talking died down and he lit all five fuses. He stepped back just in time for them to go off. They flew into the night sky, flashing around the full moon like it was exploding into little bits.

The crowd went wild as the sky erupted in color and big booms.

As quickly as the chaos of light and sound began, it died down, ending with one final punctuation.

Whistles and applause burst out through the space.

Stone glanced at Ella. She looked absolutely beautiful laying back on the grass, soaking in the good vibes. This was certainly her night and he was so glad it went the way she had hoped it would.

"Well, this is quite the shindig you have going on

here," a voice said from beyond the darkness of the tree line just behind Stone.

Stone turned to face it.

Ella was on her feet immediately, making her way to his side. Marta also joined them, her gaze locked on the woods.

A sickening feeling swelled in the pit of Stone's stomach and he forced back a snarl.

Stone knew that voice.

Nothing good came from the one who wielded it.

Suddenly, wolves burst from the forest, crashing the party, and tearing apart the serenity of the night.

CHAPTER 21

INDEPENDENCE DAY

ELLA

A different pack rushes out of the woods behind Stone and my number one priority is protecting my own.

Being caught unaware isn't my favorite thing in the world. I blame the stupid hard lemonades and the entirely happy place I'd been in for my lowered defenses.

Who expects party crashers when you're surrounded by nearly a hundred werewolves?

Seriously?

The invading pack fans out, surrounding us in a semi-circle. From what I can tell, we're outnumbered, and despite myself, fear coils in my stomach.

If it comes to a fight, I don't know if we can win this thing. My pack has only barely begun to trust me and I have no idea who's capable of what.

Shit.

Stone and Marta are instantly by my side and it's like our minds merge. Somehow, we begin sharing thoughts, feelings, and even each other's visual vantage points. It's like as a unit, we have the ability to gain a three-hundred-and-sixty-degree view by tapping into one another.

Without even speaking words or having to share thoughts, there's a simple *knowing* that passes between us.

I don't know how it all works. Only that it's incredibly helpful.

What I *do know* is this isn't the Portland Pack—it's something else.

Someone new.

"What exactly is the meaning of this?" I call out, letting the power inside me imbue my words as I stare out into the darkness.

I need this guy to know I'm not pleased.

For whatever reason, the pack's Alpha chooses to remain hidden in the shadows and I'm not digging it.

Instead of answering me, a dark, menacing laugh is all he returns.

I inhale sharply, wanting to be able to see my enemy, not imagine him. If I can see it, I can fight it.

Around us, the new pack of wolves snarls and bare their teeth.

They're definitely not here for fireworks and beers.

I glance over my shoulder and catch the terror in Avery's eyes as she clutches her brother close—no longer the TikToker with her camera ready. Thankfully, Asher holds onto her without question. He's ready to protect her, even though the two of them are the most vulnerable ones here.

Without even asking, Clementine slowly makes her way to my kids. She knows exactly what I need in order to do whatever comes next. She'll find a way to keep the kids safe, I have no doubt.

Nodding my appreciation to her, I turn back to the hidden Alpha.

"You know, if you wanted to join the party, all you had to do was ask. But this is a little rude, don't you think? We don't even have enough food," I say, drawing on my go-to defense—inappropriate and ill-timed humor.

Hey, it's better than my go-to F-response.

"And we're nearly out of beer," I continue. "So, there's that."

Finally, a man steps out of the darkness. In the moonlight, his pale skin is damned near radiant. But it's the tattoos that snake up his neck and over his bald head that give me pause. He's covered with skulls, weapons, and God knows what else.

He clearly wants to look dangerous and he does a good job of it.

"What is it with Alpha's being bald?" I mutter under my breath.

I seriously hope that isn't an ominous warning that I'm about to lose all of my hair.

Marta snickers beside me but doesn't say anything. Instead, she exudes an anticipatory level of almost...*excitement*. She wants a fight. Or maybe she's just preparing for it.

Two large wolves follow their Alpha, slinking forward from the shadows. I get the sense they're his Beta and maybe a Delta. But for sure they're leadership. Their red eyes glow on either side of him, relaying the danger that awaits us, should there be a misstep.

"I don't need your approval, *child*. I do what I want. *Take* what I want," the Alpha says, wrapping his innate power around each syllable. "So, if you know what's good for you, just sit back and let me do my thing."

His words slide across my skin, giving me all the creepy vibes.

If I thought Silas was bad news, this guy is at least his equal. They'd probably be buddies if they knew each other. Hell, for all I know, they are.

"Well, you obviously didn't hear but we're not in the market for a hostile takeover," I declare, keeping my head held high. Thankfully, my voice is more secure than I feel. "We just got rid of the last guy whose head was too big for his own good."

A renewed sense of pride about who I'm becoming —*who the pack is becoming* floods through me.

This day may have started with me feeling disconnected and anxious about everyone, but I no longer feel that way. They are all linked to me. Bound in ways I'm not even able to describe, much less understand.

I feel them now, more than ever, and they won't go down without a fight.

So, there's no way I'm going to roll over and submit.

"I don't think you have much of a choice," he says, taking another step forward. A grin spreads across his face, making me shiver in repulsion. "In case you missed it, you're severely outnumbered."

Stone grabs hold of my wrist, and his green eyes are wide when I turn to look at him.

We're gonna need to proceed with extreme caution. Derek is unhinged—like the rest of his Three Rivers Pack.

I turn back to face the new Alpha and narrow my gaze.

Derek, huh? Yeah, he looks like a Derek.

I suck in a deep breath and respond, *Kinda figured.*

Unhinged or not, after everything that's happened this past month, no one comes into *my* territory thinking we're an easy mark. I mean, we might be, but fuck them for assuming it.

Let's get this over with.

I barely have time to acknowledge my rise in energy as goosebumps flash across my body. From there, I shudder and my shift is instantaneous. I'm on four feet and heading in the direction of the one in command.

To hell with this. My kids are here. My *family* is here.

No one crashes my party expecting to take it over without one hell of a fight.

I sense the rest of the pack shift all around me, taking mine as their signal to let their animals loose.

For a sweet, brief moment, Derek's eyes widen at the sight of me and my pack as we race toward him. But before I can gloat, he's shifted into an enormous gray and black wolf. His eyes lack the red shimmer of the cronies behind him, but he's terrifying nonetheless.

I slow, shifting into a sideways prowl, as I veer slightly to the right, looking for any opening or opportunity to attack. Stone mimics me, keeping on my right flank while Marta hangs back, eyeing the Three Rivers wolves and giving me data on what's happening around us.

The rest of the pack also started incorporating their insights, funneling it up the chain of command.

Derek pivots slightly, keeping his distance, and snarling at us. Then, he launches forward with such agility that he's on me in seconds. I drop down to my back, using his momentum against him as I kick him up and over.

From there, Stone gets hold of him, latching his jaws onto Derek's neck, and tossing him back the way he had come.

Chaos erupts all around us as the Three Rivers Pack engages with mine.

I barely have time to catch Clementine's plan to get the kids out of the fray before one of Derek's red-eyed buggers catches me off guard. His jaws clamp down on the center of my spine, driving me to the ground and forcing out a yelp.

The pain doesn't last long because Stone leaps over me, knocking the wolf off and breaking me free.

I scramble back up to my feet and race at Derek with a ferocity that threatens to rip me apart.

How fucking dare he? We were having a party. There were *humans* here.

When I get to him, he rears up, raising his front paws in defense of anything I might try. I do the same, swiping at him with my claws in an attempt to gain purchase anywhere vulnerable.

I'd be happy taking an eyeball or two.

Unfortunately, he's too fast. He rolls out of the way, then slinks past me, giving us a bit of space.

We lock eyes and I swear, if we had a telepathic link, he'd be running off his villain diatribe right about now—telling me all the ways he was going to hurt me and make me suffer slowly.

Another snarl erupts from the back of my throat.

Watch his Beta, Stone warns. *He's edging closer.*

I've got him, Marta says, breaking from her location and diving headlong at him.

All around us, wolves are in similar fights. Snaps

and snarls must be heard for miles if anyone not already here is around to hear them.

Suddenly, pain tears through me—but it's not mine. It's the pain of the pack as the invaders begin to dominate my wolves.

Every slice, break, and bite come at me as if they're happening to me and I let out an ear-piercing howl, hoping to release the agony of it. For them...*and me.*

Half of my pack joins in, howling their heads off.

The sound is fucking haunting.

Shuddering the energy of it away, I race at the invading Alpha again. This time, I gain purchase on his shoulder, slamming him to the ground. He twists, rearing up and kicking me off of him like I was nothing. I roll across the grass, digging into the dirt to stop myself.

Stone hits him a second time, trying to land his teeth on the same spot I had just torn into. Unfortunately, he's intercepted by another member of their pack. They tussle, becoming nothing more than a rolling ball of fur and snarls.

Clouds roll past the moon, allowing an unhindered view of it to illuminate the field.

A shockwave of power snaps through my pack, rolling through each of us. I have no idea where it came from or why, but it gives me a boost of energy to get back into the mix.

Rather than going straight for Derek, I race off into the trees, hoping to draw him to me. If I can get him away from his pack, I have a better chance of getting the upper hand. At least going toe to toe is better than continually getting interrupted by one of his cronies.

Is she leaving us?

She's not abandoning us, is she?

Of course not, you'd feel it.

The pack's sentiments hit me like a ton of bricks but I don't have time to send them my intentions. I can only hope their faith in me isn't so easily broken.

My plan to draw Derek out did its job all too well.

He races after me, clearly hell-bent on taking me out.

He has a fierce kind of power because his speed is far superior to my own. In seconds, his jaws clamp down on my back in the same place his pack member had, causing me to buckle.

If I didn't know any better, I'd think he was trying to get me to bow down to him.

Never gonna happen.

Where the hell are you? Stone's thoughts hit me.

I tense my back muscles, then roll to the side, slamming Derek into the trunk of a tree. He lets go with a minuscule yelp.

A little busy...

You shouldn't be taking him on alone. The panic in Stone's thoughts unleash more than a little alarm inside me as he repeats, *Where are you?*

In the woods. I respond, fighting back the pain that's clawing its way down my spine.

Derek maneuvers back around, going for one of my back legs the way Silas had. I slam my ass down, driving his head to the dirt. Then, I spin around and bite down hard on the end of his muzzle.

His front paws rear up, pushing me off of him with relative ease. However, I take pleasure in the taste of his blood in my mouth.

He may be big, bad, and ugly, but I drew first blood. At least, I think I did.

A strange sensation rolls over me, setting off a host of Spidey-senses I have yet to understand. A familiar energy and scent hit me and I stop everything.

Silas?

I turn, eyeing the tree line in search of him. But as hard as I try, I can't make out anything in the darkness. It's not like I have infrared vision or something. Besides, his wolf is as black as the shadows and he's no longer a part of our pack.

If that asshole is the reason for this, so help me...

Suddenly, I'm thrown across the forest floor as Derek crashes into me. Before I can gain my bearings, his jaws clamp across my throat and squeeze.

CHAPTER 22

TWO WAYS THIS ENDS

ELLA

Desperation floods through me.

My pack is struggling to hold their ground and if I go down, everything will crumble. They'll be subjected back into the clutches of a narcissistic asshat—and that's the last thing I want for them.

I may not have a firm grip on who I am as their leader, but I know that much.

Not to mention my kids...

Oh, god.

Stone bursts through the tree line, making his way to us. His white fur is muted in the darkness under the canopy of leaves, but he's still easy to spot.

Too easy.

Derek's Beta and another wolf from their pack intercept him before he can get to me.

I struggle to break free, clawing at my attacker, but

Derek's jaws only tighten. Then he shakes his head, yanking back hard. Pain sears through my jugular and my howl of agony rips through the night.

Another try like that and I'm done for.

Stone and I need help. I broadcast the message through the pack connection, hoping like hell one of the wolves from my pack can break free to lend their aid. I don't pick any one member simply for that reason. I'll take any help I can get at this point.

My insides flutter with relief as a huge brown wolf bursts onto the scene.

Only...it's not one of my pack members.

It's *Philip.*

Confusion and concern grip me. However, he manages to take Derek by surprise, as well, and the pressure on my throat is suddenly released.

I use the opportunity to wiggle out of his vicinity and get back on my feet. My vision swims and I swing my head from side to side, trying to shake it off.

A few yards away, the two Alphas tussle, then break apart with their hackles raised. They stare at one another, each crouching low and ready to pounce.

Philip growls, baring his teeth. As nice as he was to me, he's a damn scary wolf.

Quickly, I assess the situation and turn tail to help Stone. His situation is two against one and there's no way I'm gonna let that stand.

The moon breaks free from the branches and weirdly, when it does, I feel so much better... More powerful than I had when I entered the woods and their dark embrace.

I don't have time to question it, though.

A strange sensation clenches in the center of my torso and a wave of energy bursts from me and connects to Stone. Despite having two wolves attacking him, he breaks free. They fly off of him as if a bomb had exploded.

Racing to him, I join up, standing shoulder to shoulder with my Delta. If they want to attack him, they'll have to go through both of us. Somehow, I doubt a Beta and a miscellaneous pack member are anywhere near as strong as the two of us.

Two wolves from my pack, a gray wolf and Marta, rush onto the scene ready to fight alongside us.

Suddenly, it's four against two. The Beta from the Three Rivers Pack turns, running from us, and heading toward his Alpha.

Marta, ward them off. They can't reach Derek.

Even as I release the command, I know the only way to stop this bullshit is to make Derek submit. It's the wolf way.

He needs to know I'm not about to be conquered and the Black Crater Pack is not here for the taking.

Philip and his pack might be here to help, and it's greatly appreciated, but this isn't his fight. If we're going to be left alone, I'll need to set an example with the Three Rivers Pack.

On it. Marta responds. She breaks off, intercepting them just in the nick of time.

More wolves join us in the woods, racing toward the scene like their asses are on fire. Some of them are mine, some are from the Portland Pack.

Stone, help me take down Derek.

In order to come out on top, I'll need to rely on any advantages I have. Stone's connection to me is certainly one of them.

Stone's acceptance is more of a vibe than his actual thoughts. It's like he syncs up his energy with mine as we maneuver through the trees, taking on the expanded vision that encompasses the other's viewpoint.

I reach the other Alphas first and from what I can tell, Philip is holding his own. Any attempt that Derek makes in trying to get into his personal space is thwarted.

Ella, look out. Marta's thoughts surge at me.

I turn just in time to catch a random wolf from the Three Rivers Pack launching himself from behind me. He lands hard on my back, flattening me to the ground. I roll to the side and kick him off of me.

By the time I get back up, Stone and Marta have him. Marta clamps her strong jaws over his throat and her intent to end him comes across loud and clear.

Don't kill him. I command, making my way to her.

As assholeish of a move this has been, I understand this is how they think things are done. Survival of the fittest, and all that.

Marta stops, flitting her golden eyes to me.

Keep him subdued. I turn from her and face Derek. Stone is already creeping around the other side of him, ready to make his move.

An unearthly sound gathers in the back of my throat and I unleash a howl infused with power. Stone joins in, matching the melody of it, and my heart beams.

Our entire pack rallies, joining into the mix. Their howl is breathtaking and their energy immediately picks up as they return to whatever it was they were doing. Only, they have more focus—*more impact.*

I return my gaze to Derek, prowling forward.

Stone edges around the other side of him, ensuring he has nowhere to run.

Interestingly, Philip backs off, giving us space to do our thing. He hovers just off to the right, keeping tabs on the situation, I have no doubt.

I appreciate his help and his acceptance of what we want here.

Tunnel vision takes over and my only goal is to neutralize this new threat, so I can free my pack from his onslaught. They didn't deserve this.

Derek backs away, clearly trying to keep the two of us in front of him. Smart move.

However, Stone and I work as one unit, somehow communicating on a level that transcends conscious thought. We don't need to communicate that way—it's too slow.

Instead, it's all instinct. Instantaneous perception beyond words.

I lunge for Derek as Stone circles around to the back of him. Derek bows down as I get near, but I manage to latch onto the side of his neck. I tug hard, shaking my head from side to side in the hopes of disorienting him enough to get a chance at his throat.

I want him to feel the same panic I felt.

Unfortunately, he's fast and twists out of my grip before I can do much.

He immediately turns his attention to Stone. With more power than I've seen him summon, he rushes my Delta, using his shoulder to knock him sideways and into a tree.

Stone hits with a sickening crack, not even letting out a cry.

My heart seizes. *Is he okay?*

Derek doesn't wait to find out, he pounces on top of Stone, trying to get access to his jugular.

With as much power as I can muster, I slam into him, latching onto the meaty part of his back leg. Then, I drag him backward and practically toss him off of Stone.

Derek twists, snapping his jaws at me as he tries to catch the side of my face with his teeth. Thankfully, he only catches air as I drop him and back up.

A snarl of anger rips from my lips.

Stone gets back on his feet and relief washes through me.

While Derek's focused on me, Stone attacks him from the left. His teeth dig deep into the side of the Alpha's shoulder, forcing a cry from him. The stench of blood floods my nostrils and I know the bite has done damage.

In the distance, Marta lets out a shriek, and her desperation slams into me like a physical force.

I turn just as the Beta from the Three Rivers Pack takes a chunk out of the left side of her face. His eyes flash with malice and his muzzle is covered in her blood. She recoils, dropping down and covering her face with her front paws.

The Beta goes feral, continuing to lash out, biting and clawing at her with fervor.

Anger rises in a new wave and I fight the urge to drop everything I'm doing to seek revenge.

Instead, I launch a command to have anyone with the ability to help Marta.

I have to end this once and for all.

Derek takes the distraction as an opportunity to get out of Stone's grip and make a run for it.

He weaves in and out of trees as he tries to put some distance between us.

Stone and I race after him. We stay on his tail, focused on matching his every move. He veers off to the right, heading toward what looks like a large open field.

Apprehension grips me.

If this is a trap...

Ultimately, it doesn't matter if it is.

There are only two ways this ends and quitting isn't one of them.

Moonlight bathes the field, illuminating a sea of little white flowers that cover the space. It's the kind of beauty I'd enjoy reveling in if the situation wasn't so dire.

As soon as we hit the clearing, I get another surge of energy. It's like every cell of my body renews itself—healing and giving me more clarity.

Stone and I glow with an odd vibrance that continues to pump energy into us both. Again, it's like the moon herself is smiling down on me, lending her magic and support the second her gaze is unhindered.

I know it sounds stupid, but that's how it feels.

Crazier yet, I think Stone feels it, too.

He rushes into the clearing and our connection heightens.

Somehow, it like we're two halves of the same whole. Feeling what the other is feeling, seeing what the other is seeing.

Maybe this is how it always is... But it's new to me.

Without any extra effort, we catch up to Derek. Stone bites onto the left side of his neck and as the Alpha twists to fight him off, I clamp down on his right side.

Together, our attack is enough to make Derek lose

his footing. He goes down like a fallen elk, and face-first into the flowers. He skids across the grass, leaving a trail of blood in the flattened field behind him.

I step forward, slamming my front paws against Derek's throat.

White-hot anger sears through me and my body quivers as I decide just how far I'm going to take this.

The packs begin to gather, no longer engaging in their own fights, as they join to witness our battle. It's like they know this is the end of things and they need to be here.

There's a peculiar sentiment that rolls through each of them—but it's not something I understand. Nor is it something we have time for.

I bend down, barring my teeth and barely containing a growl.

A knowing overcomes me and I know without a shadow of a doubt this will be the end of him.

I'll make sure he never tries something like this again.

This is *my* home. *My* pack.

An intense vibration takes over my being as the power in me and through my pack rises.

Suddenly, Derek is no longer in his wolf form. Instead, he lays naked and bleeding in the dirt in front of us. Slowly, he raises his hands in the air, keeping his eyes trained down. "I submit."

CHAPTER 23

GOOD RIDDANCE

ELLA

Almost as if a switch is flipped, all fighting comes to a complete stop.

I hover over Derek, fighting the adrenaline coursing through me and debating if I should take him out anyway.

Philip is the second wolf to shift back into his human form. Then, one by one, the field of flowers is full of naked humans. Some are bloody and battered, while others are simply disheveled and alert.

The now-familiar static electricity rises inside me, making each strand of fur stand on end. Then, as quickly as it comes, I'm human, and kneeling in the field like a friggin' superhero.

My nostrils flare as I stand up and glare at Derek.

"Get out of my territory," I ground out.

Power threads through each syllable and he shudders from its intensity. Thankfully, he keeps his trap shut.

Philip steps forward, his head held high. "I will take care of the Three Rivers Pack and ensure they return to their territory. That is, if you approve."

My gaze slides to his and I hold it for a beat. He's proud, for sure, but his proclamation holds no assumption. I appreciate that.

Without saying anything, I tip my head in approval.

If we can get both packs out of my area, all the better.

Stone is suddenly behind me on the left-hand side. He places a warm hand on my shoulder and leans in. "We should send a few from our pack with them to ensure their compliance."

I nod. "Agreed. Stone, you can choose the ones you think would be best. I trust your judgment"

"Sure," he says with a quick tip of his chin.

Derek rises slowly, his eyes still trained on the ground. I don't know if it's shame or simply a part of the process. Either way, he doesn't meet my gaze.

Instead, he turns to face Philip, who puffs his chest in response.

The Portland Alpha raises an arm, pointing to the purple-haired chick that had cornered me in the bathroom. "Stay put. Zara, keep him in check. I must speak with Ella."

Purple-hair nods, wrapping her fingers around Derek's bicep.

The Three Rivers Alpha heaves a sigh. I can only see his backside, but I swear his energy is bordering agitation.

He's clearly not used to getting bested by women.

Granted, I think I'd be agitated, too, if I was forced to submit. Regardless of who made me do it.

"Ella, we should also attend to Marta. Her wounds need to be looked at," Stone whispers.

I turn to him, fear suddenly gripping me.

He shakes his head and raises a hand. "It's just superficial but if she doesn't get her bite looked at soon, she'll scar. I doubt she'll appreciate that."

"Oh, right. Let's get Seth on it," I say, delegating to the best person I know to handle the situation.

He nods, then vanishes from my periphery.

I breathe a sigh of relief because for whatever reason, despite having just been in the heat of battle, my body reacts to his naked proximity. There's no way I let myself turn around to watch him go, either, because I'd just stare. Drool would probably be involved and I doubt that would go well at the present moment.

Philip takes me by the elbow, drawing me to the side. "Ella, I want you to know that you and your pack fought...*valiantly*."

There's an odd reverence that coats his words and

it pulls me up short. "I was just protecting what was mine."

He tips his head. "As you should." For a moment, his dark eyes search mine, then his eyebrows pinch together and he continues, "I feel I should also express... When I came here, it was with the utmost respect for you and your pack. It may not have appeared that way but you must know I believe women are powerful. They should also be respected. My pack has taught me that much. So, with that in mind, I want to reiterate that although I wish you would reconsider joining us, I will respect your decision for autonomy. Should you need our help again, simply say the word. Please consider the Portland Pack an ally."

"Thank you, Philip. I appreciate that," I say, smiling softly. "And no, I'm not going to change my mind. But thank you for the offer."

"After witnessing moon wolves in action, I understand why you would wish to remain loyal to your own," he says.

His weird reverence is back and I shoot him a sideways glance.

"Uhm, thank you?" I say, my words coming out as more of a question than I meant to.

Rather than explaining himself, he turns to face Derek and his purple-haired barbarian. "It is time for us to be leaving. I am glad I was here to witness today's events."

With that, he saunters off. His dark skin glimmers in the moonlight and unlike with Stone, I'm already facing Derek as he meanders away. I can't help but marvel at the sheer amount of muscle he carries on him. And yet, he still doesn't spark the reactions Stone does simply by being near me.

The Portland Pack shifts into their wolf forms, triggering the Three Rivers wolves to do the same. I stand there in the middle of the field, watching them all fade into the tree line and out of sight.

When they're all gone, and only my pack remains, I release the breath I was holding.

How the hell did we dodge another bullet?

For a moment, I was sure we were going down—and it would have all been my fault. People were warning me that other packs could make a move. But instead of listening, I was too focused on handling things like a human would have.

I should have realized shit was about to go sideways. Things had gone sooooo good.

Too good.

It should have been the slap in the face I needed to be on guard. Nothing goes that well in my world without turning into a shitshow.

Thankfully, things turned out okay.

Granted, there are wounded...

Shit. *Marta.*

I turn around, searching for my Beta. Ironically, while I can feel her general location, it's Seth's red hair that catches my attention. Then, I notice Stone, kneeling beside her.

Rushing in their direction, I ignore the small rocks and twigs that dig into the bottoms of my feet now that I'm in human form. I hadn't even registered them at all when I was a wolf.

"How is she doing?" I ask, kneeling down on the other side of her.

Stone glances up, smiling at me. I can't help but notice he keeps his eyes north of my neck.

"I've done what I can from here but I need to get her to the house. Stone has more medical supplies there," Seth says, leaning back.

Marta rolls her eyes. "I'll be fine. I'm sure I've been through worse. You guys are making a fuss over nothing."

"Let me see," I say, leaning around to get a better look.

She turns her head to face me.

A large gash from the bottom of her left eye to her lip has been torn wide open. Its angry, jagged skin is already trying to weave itself back together, but it looks gnarly.

Despite myself, I shudder.

"Well, you could have at least tried to hide it." Marta laughs.

Thank God she has a sense of humor about it. I'd be freaking the fuck out right about now.

"Sorry. I've never been any good with blood. Just

ask my kids," I say, sticking out my tongue. "It freaks me out."

"Well, I have a feeling you're going to need to get used to the sight of it," Seth says, wincing slightly.

I pat him on the shoulder. "That is *not* what I wanna hear."

He chuckles under his breath and nods.

The kids.

My brain pings and I turn back toward the direction of Stone's property. Clementine had taken them on, and I know she'd keep them safe if she could. However, I shouldn't assume anything.

I should have checked.

Clementine? Are the kids—? I reach out, connecting to her directly. Without waiting for her to respond, I stand up and shift back into my wolf form.

Not even letting anyone know why I abruptly left, I race through the forest.

They're fine. With all the chaos, I was able to get them to Stone's bunker. Clementine's response reaches me. *How are things there? Has the fighting stopped?*

Relief slams into me but I continue running anyway. Without a pack connection to my kids, the only way I'll feel better is to see them and feel them for myself.

The other packs are leaving. Derek submitted.

Pack members who are not helping the wounded or leading the Three Rivers Pack out of our territory follow after me. I haven't broadcast a need or a reason for them to do so, but I feel them joining me regardless.

Maybe they know the party is over and it's time to go home.

Stone's wolf is suddenly running alongside me. He hasn't asked why I ran off, but I have a feeling he already knows. He seems to understand me on a deeper level than most. Together, we race side-by-side, soaking in the moonlight. Somehow, we're energized by it and even by each other.

By the time we break from the forest and back onto Stone's lawn, the lights from his house guide the way. My kids must be okay because every light in the house is on.

When I reach his back porch, I shift back into my human form and rush into the house.

"Avery—Asher?" I call out. "Clementine?"

Both kids poke their heads into the kitchen from the hallway.

"Is it over?" Avery asks, her voice still higher than normal. "Clementine said it was over..."

I nod and walk over to her. "Yes, sweetie. It's over."

Asher's eyes are trained on the ceiling as he says, "I *knew* you'd kick their asses."

I shake my head. "Well, you were definitely in the minority there, kid. I wasn't sure of anything at first."

"Mom, are you kidding? As soon as I saw you transform, or whatever... You were—" Asher says, his brown eyes wide as he drops his gaze to me, "*fucking awesome.*"

I lower my eyebrows. "Asher."

He shakes his head. "Sorry, Mom. But there's no other way to describe it. I'm so glad we got to witness it this time. It makes the whole naked thing not matter so much."

I glance down, realizing I had forgotten all about the clothing aspect. "Well, I'm thrilled, but—"

"I want you to bite me," he proclaims, holding out an arm and walking toward me.

My mouth drops open and my heart leaps into my throat. I throw his arm back at him. "Are you serious right now?"

"Yeah, Mom. I am. What you did was so epic," he says, excitement and admiration clear in his tone. "I wanna be like you."

"Forget epic. Did you not see how dangerous things were? How *dire?*" I sputter.

"In case you didn't catch it, things were pretty dire for us humans, too," he says, jutting out his chin. "At least you guys could protect yourself. We had to run and hide like babies. If I were a part of your pack, maybe I could do more than just cower in a basement every time something goes sideways."

"We are not having this conversation. Not after a night like tonight," I fire back, then walk away from him.

"This is *exactly* the right time to talk about this. I could have helped—"

"Hell *no*," I say, spinning back to him. Without meaning to, I infuse the words with an Alpha command and both Clementine and Stone snap their attention to me as they enter the room. One from the depths of the house, the other behind me. I pinch the bridge of my nose. "No, Asher. I won't allow it."

His face pinches tight and his cheeks flame. "Yeah, we'll see. I'm eighteen soon. Then what are you gonna do?"

CHAPTER 24

IT JUST FIGURES

ELLA

I stare at Asher in disbelief.

It just figures.

I can make another Alpha cry uncle but I can't seem to manage to scare the living daylights out of my own son.

What am I gonna do when he turns eighteen?

Lock him in Stone's bunker indefinitely comes to mind.

But I don't say anything.

Instead, I bite my lip to keep it from quivering.

This is the last thing I'd ever want for Asher.

He has his whole life ahead of him. I would never want to condemn him to *this* life.

Even if having a pack link to him would be handy...

No, he needs a normal life and I'll do everything in my power to make sure he gets exactly that.

I spin on my heel, turning my back to him and toward the door.

"Now you've done it, *stupid*," Avery hisses.

Spinning around, I glare at her from under my eyebrows. "Avery."

She stands up straighter and frowns. "Sorry. You're not stupid." Then she sticks out her tongue. "Just *dumb*."

I run my hand over my face.

Lord help me.

Huffing a sigh, I exit the building.

The kids are safe for now. *Granted, Asher's days might be numbered...*

But there's one last thing to take care of.

"Party's over, guys. Thanks so much for coming," I say, trying desperately to ignore the fact that I'm standing in the middle of Stone's deck buck-ass naked and surrounded by plenty of other buck-ass naked people.

If someone wandered by they'd think we had a goddamn orgy in this backyard. And trust, that would have been more fun than how this night ended.

"Is it over?" Someone calls out from the middle of the yard.

I turn to face the source, connecting to the inner-knowing that it came from Cora, the girl who'd been talking with Asher. "Yes, it's over. The pack who attacked—they're being escorted out of our territory."

Relief and murmurs pass through the pack.

"Now, don't get me wrong. We may have won things tonight, but it was by the skin of our teeth. If the Portland Pack hadn't come to our aid—" I begin, still reeling from the events. "Things may have ended very differently. Going forward, I'm going to need the help of each of you. I don't want us to be blindsided like this again. So, I need to get up to speed on the nearby packs and understand the rules. But for now, go home. Heal up. You did good."

I stand there, watching as the pack members turn to each other. Some break off in conversations, others start picking up items in the yard, and others outright leave.

Marta and Seth make their appearance from the woods. Then, when they get closer, they wave as they head inside Stone's house. My heart constricts at the sight of her face and I pray to the moon—or any deity who might listen—to take care of her.

Inhaling the crisp night air, I continue to stand on the deck and watch as the numbers dwindle down to only a handful. When the last of the pack has left, or gone inside, I turn my gaze to the moon.

Her full face shines down on me and a low hum vibrates through my core. I stare at my hand, turning it over. Just like when I was in wolf form, even my skin has an eerie glow in the moonlight tonight.

I don't understand it yet, but I can feel its signifi-cance. There's something powerful going on between me and the moon. Hell, between Stone and the moon, too.

And I intend to find out what it means.

As if on cue, the skin along my backside hums and Stone approaches. He drapes his warm hands against my hips, pulling me to the front of his body.

Without even turning around, I can tell he put clothes on. Probably for my benefit—or maybe for my kids.

I lean into him, allowing his strength to permeate through to me.

"Hell of a night, huh?" he finally says, his breath brushing against the side of my neck.

I snicker under my breath. "Truer words have never been spoken."

"You handled yourself incredibly well," he says, his voice a low rumble.

"Yeah, so well that I didn't even notice an adversary was closing in. I thought I was meant to have some sort of sixth sense, Stone. Why didn't I realize—" I begin, turning around to face him.

His dark eyebrows knit together. "Ella, you were enjoying yourself. And to be fair, *no one* realized they were there. I didn't even sense them until it was too late."

"So, what does that mean?" I ask, acutely aware that I'm standing beside him completely naked while he's clad in shorts and a white t-shirt.

He shrugs. "I'm not sure. Maybe nothing."

"But maybe something?" I ask.

"Maybe?"

I release a sigh and pinch the bridge of my nose. There's so much about this life I don't really understand yet. So much I wish I could parse apart and examine.

It's fascinating and scary. Not to mention exhilarating and annoyingly complex.

But tomorrow, when the sun rises, I have to focus on reality again.

I need to find a new job. I need to keep my family safe.

"What are you thinking about?" Stone asks, running his palms down the sides of my arms and making me shudder.

"Just that... I wish things were easier," I whisper, dropping the top of my head to his chest.

He wraps his arms around my shoulders and stands there for a moment, just holding me. "Things will get easier."

I snort into his shirt. "Yeah, right. Did you not hear Asher a few minutes ago? My life is never going to get easier."

Stone crooks a finger and tips my chin upward until I have no choice but to look into his eyes. "Asher will be fine. He's a young man looking to find his place in this world. Give him time. He'll be on to his next big idea," Stone says with a ghost of a smile.

"You say that like it's coming from experience."

"Maybe a little. Granted, I was the other way around," he says, huffing out a laugh.

"What's so funny?" I ask, searching his eyes.

His eyebrows flick upward. "Well, before you... I had dedicated my life to finding a cure for *this*. But now, it doesn't seem so important. I'm wondering what my next big idea will be."

I suck in a breath, realizing this is the first time I really got what he did for a living.

If I could, would I give all of this up?

Surprisingly, my emotions are conflicted about the concept.

"Ella, this might not be the right time, but to hell with it," Stone says, suddenly serious. He drops my arms to take a step back from me and pace.

I quirk an eyebrow, anxious to find out what's got him so antsy.

He stops pacing and says, "In werewolf packs, there's this...*thing*."

"Thing?" I ask, narrowing my gaze. My heart thumbs unevenly in my chest as I wait for his next response.

He nods. "It's rare, but when it happens, it's—" He blows out a puff of air.

"What is it?" I ask, stepping toward him.

His eyes flit to me and he says, "Do you believe in fate?"

I shrug. "Sure."

"No, I mean, the kind of fate you couldn't fight

even if you tried. The kind that's so powerful, you're helpless against it," he asks, his eyes now pleading with me.

"I don't understand," I mutter, shaking my head.

"In werewolf packs, sometimes couples are destined for one another. We call them *fated mates,*" he says, the final two words dropping into a whisper.

I narrow my eyes, considering his words. Something in them resonates with me like a magical spell that weaves in and out of my mind.

"Fated mates?" I repeat.

Stone nods.

"Are you saying you think we—" I point from me to him and back again.

Again, he nods. "Do you feel it?"

Glancing at the moon, I suck in a breath.

I *do* feel it.

There's a connection to him that just pulls me to him. It makes me want to be with him in ways I've never been with anyone. But more than that, I feel more powerful, more connected when I'm with him.

My tongue skates across my lower lip and I nod.

"That's what Philip was getting at the other day. Wolves, when we pair up, we call it mating," he smiles softly. "I guess we try to stay true to our animals that way. But mating isn't so much like marriage. It's deeper than that."

"We claim each other?" I say, realization hitting home.

His eyes widen and his nostrils flare. "Yes."

I blink wildly, trying to process this new information.

"There's more," he says, eyeing me closely.

I chuckle darkly. "Of course, there is."

"I don't know what it means, but I think we owe it to ourselves to find out," he says, running a fingertip over his eyebrow.

I hold my breath, waiting for the shoe to drop.

Fated mates and claiming are one thing...

"There are legends of *moon wolves*. I honestly don't know them all that well. They've been garbled through the ages," he begins. "However, after tonight, I'm beginning to wonder if we might be..."

"Moon wolves," I whisper. "Philip said something like that. Something about seeing Moon Wolves in action—"

"When?" Stone asks.

"Right before he left," I say, pointing to the woods as if it's an explanation of where we were.

He narrows his eyes, then nods to himself.

"So," I breathe, "we have a lot to excavate."

Stone's lips twitch into a smile and he steps forward. "There's no one I'd rather be with to uncover the truth...*than you.*"

My heart flutters and my body reacts, tightening things in ways the night's chill hadn't yet managed.

Stone raises a hand, brushing his knuckles across my cheek, then he tucks a wisp of hair behind my ear.

"Ella, if there's one thing this past week has thrown into sharp perspective, it's..." he pauses, dropping his gaze to my lips. He trails his fingertips over my clavicle, invoking goosebumps to scatter across my skin. "From the moment I met you, I was drawn to you. I couldn't explain it and didn't know what it meant at first. But if we're *fated*..."

My insides flip and I try desperately to ignore the heat from his body as it radiates against mine. "What are you saying?" I breathe.

He smirks in the slowest, sexiest way and it sets my lady bits on fire. "Are you free tomorrow?" His emerald eyes sparkle in the moonlight as he watches me intensely. "I'd like to take you on a date. Maybe if you're good, I'll even *claim you.*"

CHAPTER 25
SIDETRACKED

ELLA

I don't understand why this is so nerve-wracking. I'm the Alpha of a werewolf pack, for crying out loud. I've fought for my life—*multiple times.*

Yet, no matter how hard I try, the idea of going on an official date with Stone is absolutely terrifying. And *exhilarating.*

I bite my lower lip, drop the red dress, and swap it out for the blue one. I hold it up against my body and stare at my reflection in the enormous full-length mirror of the department store.

I've been here for an hour and I'm still no closer to making a choice.

"Oh, god no... Go with the red one," Jinx says, hobbling up to me from behind a rack of dresses. "It draws out the red in your hair."

Startled, I just stare at her. The last thing I was expecting was an audience.

She winks at me. "Plus, you'll look hot in it. Trust me."

My cheeks flame, but I swap out the dresses again and tilt my head to the side.

She's right. The red is better.

"Thanks, Jinx. I needed that. I was at a complete loss," I say, sliding the blue one on the return rack.

"It's what I *live* for," she says, exaggerating the word and puffing up her chest.

For whatever reason, she sounds like Ursula from *The Little Mermaid.*

I snicker softly. "Well, we seem to be running into each other a lot lately. What are you doing here? Are you on the hunt for new clothes, too?"

She scrunches her face. "Actually, I was on the hunt for *you*."

"Me?" I repeat, unable to hide my surprise. "Everything okay?"

"Psh, yeah. Everything's fine. I hope you don't mind my intrusion. I was told by some mini-me's who look suspiciously like you that I could find ya here," she says.

"Well, considering you helped me make this monumental decision, I'd say we're square. What's up?" I ask, draping the red dress over my left arm.

She points to the seating area. "Got a sec?"

"Oh boy," I mutter, eyeing the bench nervously.

"It's nothing bad. I just have a proposition for you. I've been trying to find a way to ask you for the past week, but I don't think the universe was agreeing on my timing," she says, her lips twisting into a grin.

"Hmmm...*intrigue*," I say, narrowing my gaze and taking a seat. Then, I raise my palm and flick my fingertips. "Okay, hit me up."

She makes her way over to me, and with a little bit of effort, takes a seat. "I doubt you know this, but I run a local adventure magazine and Youtube channel. It's called *The Sidetracked Scene*..."

I chuckle softly. "It sounds like it should be the title to your autobiography."

"That's fair," she responds, nodding her approval. "At any rate, I'm in the market for a new writer. This one's burning out." She jabs a thumb toward herself. "Basically, I need some fresh perspectives and I thought, maybe you'd be up for the challenge. Whatdya say? Need a little more chaos in your life?"

I blink back in my astonishment. "I—I don't know what to say."

She shrugs. "Say yes."

"Yes! Of course, I'll write for you," I sputter, reaching out and wrapping my arms around her neck.

The hanger from the dress smacks Jinx in the back of her head on the way around, then as I try to pull back and apologize, it clings onto her flaming red hair like it's holding on for dear life.

"Oh, my god, Jinx. I'm so sorry," I cry.

She reaches up, dislodging the hanger and trying not to laugh. "Looks like you bring your own chaos."

I cover my mouth, sniffling a laugh. "Looks like I do."

"Well, this outta be interesting," Jinx snickers, sliding her hands between her knees.

"That could be a gross underrepresentation of the pandemonium we're about to unleash." I shake my head, surprised by the sudden turn of events. "I can't tell you how relieved I am. My boss wasn't happy I was taking so long and he let me go. I thought I was going to have to go back to being a waitress or something."

"Well, his loss is my gain," Jinx beams.

"It certainly is. And I promise I don't normally take long to write—"

She holds up a hand. "No need to explain, Ella. I already know enough about you to understand what was going on there."

I set the dress in my lap this time and reach around, giving Jinx a squeeze. "Thank you. Seriously, *thank you.*"

"Don't thank me yet. You don't know what the assignments are gonna be."

Leaning back, I shake my head. "Anything has to be better than erectile dysfunction."

She rolls her eyes to the ceiling and pretends to think about it. "Yeah, I think you might be right there."

I nod vigorously. "So, when would you like for me to start? I'm getting ready for a date right now..." I lift the dress.

"Lord, I'm desperate, but not *that* desperate. Go on

your date. Enjoy yourself," Jinx says, slapping my knee. "So, how about we start next Monday? We can meet up at the coffee shop if you want. Nine sound good?"

"I'd love that. Thank you," I repeat.

"Woman, if you thank me one more time..."

"Sorry. Sorry," I say, holding my hands up in surrender.

"Awesome. Whew, that's a relief," Jinx mutters, leaning her back against the wall. "I didn't have a backup plan in case you said no."

Despite myself, I laugh.

Never in a million years would I have been able to see this offer coming. But one thing's for sure, turning it down was never gonna be an option.

"Well, deary... You better get ready for that hot date," she says, using my knee to lean on as she pushes herself to a stand. "I'm gonna go have a hot date with my editorial calendar. I've gotta get prepped before my new hire thinks I'm a disorganized, chaotic mess."

I giggle at the thought of her being anything but a disorganized, chaotic mess.

"See ya Monday," she says, shooting me a wink.

I nod. "See you Monday."

As she disappears through the racks of clothes, I stand up and gather my things feeling even more light-hearted than before.

I mean, going on a date with Stone was reason enough to celebrate. But now...

My insides are a flurry of activity and I'm excited

for what my future brings.

It's like everything is opening up wide and welcoming me into a crazy new world.

Well, crazier than it already was.

The drive home is a complete blur as I'm drawn into thoughts about all that's gone on. From being bitten to meeting Stone, to becoming Alpha... Then, to everything that's happened recently.

Never in a million years would I have been able to predict the direction my life would take by moving out to Oregon. But I am so thrilled I listened to Denise and took the leap.

Warts and all, I wouldn't change a thing.

When I get home, the nervous energy is back. Settling in my stomach and pinging around like a bird trapped inside my ribcage.

I set to work, getting ready for my first date since the divorce—and the first date in at least a decade. The ex would have rather spent time in front of his TV than go do something with me.

In a weird way, I feel like I'm a teenager all over again.

I pull out my curling iron and makeup—neither of which typically see the light of day. For an hour, I take my time, trying to get every detail *just right*.

It isn't until I'm putting the finishing touches on my makeup that I realize some of the nervous energy isn't even mine.

It's Stone's, too.

I stop what I'm doing to lean into the sensation. Just like me, he's getting ready and hoping things go well. I don't pry into his mind but his feelings come through loud and clear. They mimic my own in so many ways.

My heart melts in the knowledge that he's just as nervous as I am. He wants to make a good impression on me in the same way I want to for him.

I don't know what I did to get so lucky, but I'll certainly take it.

Placing my makeup back in its drawer, I walk from the bathroom to the bedroom to get dressed. I tug off my tank top and capris, placing them on the end of my bed for tomorrow. Then, I unhook my bra, tucking it underneath them.

Turning around, I reach out for the dress, which is now hanging on the back of the closet door.

My stomach bursts into butterflies as I sense Stone on the move.

He's on his way here.

Practically squealing in delight, I step into the dress, pulling it up and hooking the straps over my arms. The delicate fabric clings to my body in all the right ways, making me feel beautiful. That's a feeling I haven't tapped into for a very long time.

A quick knock on my bedroom door is the only warning I get before it swings open.

"Oooh, that dress is amazing," Avery says, her jaw-dropping open.

I lower my eyebrows. "Wait for a response next time."

"Whoops. Sorry," she says, making a face.

I wave her over. "Well, since you're here, help me with this zipper, would you? Stone's on his way."

"Sure," she says, walking over to me.

I turn around, pulling my hair out of the way as she zips me up.

"Thanks, sweetheart." I turn around to face her.

"Wow," Asher says from the doorway. "You look nice."

"Right?" Avery says.

I grin like the Cheshire Cat, feeling like I could absolutely take on the world.

"Mom, I'm really happy for you," Asher says, sliding his hands into his pockets.

Avery nods. "Me, too. Stone's nice. And Clementine is cool."

My heart squishes and I open my arms, inviting them in. "Thank you, guys. Your blessing means a lot to me. I mean, I have no idea what's happening or where it's leading... It's just—"

"For crying out loud, Mom. It's a date. Let it be a date for now," Asher says, snickering as he comes in for the hug. "You're not marrying the guy."

I inhale sharply, thinking back to what Stone said about the claiming process... How it's deeper than marriage. And if we are fated mates...

Something to explain another day.

Instead of voicing any of that, I just smile. "You're right. One step at a time."

"Atta girl," Asher says, patting me on the back.

Avery leans in, giving me another hug. "I can't believe our little girl is all grown up." She takes a step back, pretending to wipe a tear from her eye.

"Oh brother," I say, rolling my eyes to the ceiling. But internally, I can't help but feel so incredibly grateful.

This is the way I always wanted my life to be.

Full of adventure. Full of love. And joy...

And sex. *Sex would be nice.*

Nervous energy pools in my midsection and it combines with what feels like Stone's again, as well.

Maybe he's as excited and nervous as I am about what could take place tonight?

Will we go back to his place?

One step at a time, Ella...

The doorbell rings and I bite my lip to keep it from quivering.

"There he is," Asher says.

"Be good. Don't do anything I wouldn't do," Avery chides in.

I narrow my gaze. "There's not a lot of things you can do without being grounded for life."

"Exactly," she says, pointing at me and pretending to shoot.

Shaking my head, I grab my shoes and slide them on my feet.

"I'll keep you posted on my plans as they unfold. There's pizza money on the counter." I walk past them both and blow them a kiss.

"Have fun," Asher says, walking out onto the second-floor landing and looking over the rail.

Avery joins him and waves.

I clench my fists and give a little excited jiggle before I grab my purse and place it under my arm.

Feeling better than I have in ages and ready to face the future, I swing open the door.

"Hey, I'm—" I begin, but my smile fades and my mouth slacks open. Anything else I had planned to say dies on my lips.

Standing on my front porch isn't Stone.

It's my ex-husband, Troy.

His brown eyes flash and a triumphant smirk slides across his lips. "I'm here to see the kids."

To be continued...

DID YOU LIKE *MIDLIFE WOLF PACK?*

If so, sing your praises, my friend. No, you don't have to put on a jester's hat or do a TikTok video (though, that would be cool).

All ya gotta do is leave a review.

MIDLIFE WOLF MATE

ACCIDENTAL ALPHA · BOOK 3

Midlife can go to hell.

I can't believe he showed up here... *the ex.*

Right when things are getting good—like I might actually have this whole Alpha thing under control—*good.*

Or I'm ready to go on a date with the hottest guy I've laid eyes on—*so good he could melt my panties off*—**good**.

But now, the ex is here, throwing his weight around, and pulling all the shots with me and the kids. (Who, by the way, are as excited about his arrival as I am.)

Worst of all, I have to take it, smile pretty, and pretend as though I couldn't snap him in half with my wolfish super-strength. Because, let's face it, him finding out about my new world would be the end of it.

I never thought I'd miss the days when Silas was the big bad.

I gotta get my ex out of town or this new Alpha's gonna summon some hellfire, the likes of which this pack has never seen.

Now available!

Start Reading Now!

A NOTE FROM THE AUTHOR

Thanks so much for reading **Midlife Wolf Pack**, Book 2 in the *Accidental Alpha* series.

This series continues with *Midlife Wolf Mate* - available now!

Join my Patreon to read my books as they're being written (including this series!), get exclusive merch, and get more news and book-related nerdery from me.

Thanks for being here!
xo Carissa

CAN'T WAIT FOR MORE ACCIDENTAL ALPHA?

If you're waiting for the next installment of Accidental Alpha, check out Carissa's other series.

The Windhaven Witches

Secret Legacy

Soul Legacy

Haunted Legacy

Cursed Legacy

The Diana Hawthorne Series

The Final Five (prequel)

Oracle

Amends

Immortals

Ruins

The Pendomus Chronicles

Trajectory (prequel)

Pendomus

Polarities

Revolutions

Stand Alone Titles

Awakening

Merciless

About the Author

Carissa Andrews
Sci-fi/Fantasy is my pen of choice.

Carissa Andrews is an award-winning and international bestselling indie author from central Minnesota. Her books range from paranormal and urban fantasy to science fiction dystopia. Her plans for right now include the continuation of her acclaimed _Diana Hawthorne Supernatural Mysteries_ and a new series called _Accidental Alpha_. As a publishing powerhouse, she keeps sane by chilling with her husband, five kids, and their adorable husky, Aztec.

For a free ebook and to find out what Carissa's up to, head over to her website and sign up for her newsletter:

www.carissaandrews.com

patreon.com/carissaandrews

amazon.com/author/carissaandrews

bookbub.com/authors/carissa-andrews

goodreads.com/Carissa_Andrews